I0733208

C. H. DARKLING

CRUEL CINDERELLA

ISBN : 978-1-911424-77-2
SKU/ID: 9781911424772

Editor: Monica Turoni
Cover and Book design by: Wolf

Publishing Company:
Black Wolf Edition & Publishing Ltd.

PREFACE

C.H. Darkling, at her debut novel, brings you to discover a tainted tale dedicated to the protagonist of one of the most popular fairy tales of all time. In the first book of the trilogy, will Cinderella remain a sweet country Nobel? Will she become the Queen?
You reader will discover why she is called Cinderella and what she really hides. You will be introduced to the life and intrigues at the court of the kingdom of the King of Spain, together with his friends and enemies. A detailed description of the other characters before the real story begins will introduce you to the opening scene of the noble life of Cinderella after the loss of her mother and the acquaintance of her "new" stepmother and sisters.

The Editor

INTRODUCTION TO CHARACTERS

"Cinderella"
(Frella Ozuna / Lead Character)

Looks: age 17; very dark, strawberry blonde, extremely long and wavy hair; skin so extremely fair that it glistened nearly glowing; bright emerald green eyes.
Cinderella was absolutely beautiful; tall in height for a woman and voluptuous.

Personality: Cinderella was vain, manipulative and spiteful. She had values of loyalty and believed in keeping her word. However, if you broke yours she was as vengeful as they come. She believed in her vengeance and suffering. And, being a natural born ruler she enjoyed having the upper hand and controlling all around her. Although she had class, style and intelligence her Cinderboy indeed made her lusty.

Background: Cinderella was born into status of the richest and most prominent Nobel Families in Spain. Her mother and father were kind and honorable people. It is hard to be said if Cinderella's mother, and light of her life, dying young completely made her deranged or if it only gave her the push she needed? Some people are just born evil…was she? Regardless when her mother died, at age 12 Cinderella was left to her own devices and rule the mansion while Father was away. She in that time became wicked and was seduced by her Cinderboy at age 15 fueling her dark nature.

"Mother"
(Davina Ozuna / Cinderella's Mother)

Looks: died at age 31; dark, strawberry blonde hair; brown eyes; skin so fair it glistened.
She was beautiful like a goddess with a glowing aura everyone could see due to her heart of gold.

Personality: She was truly gentle and kind, caring for others more than herself. She was also very educated, for her station, and was very gifted in gardening, baking, art and the game of Chess.

Background: Davina came from a lower-class of bakers and gardeners. Her family married her to the Ozuna's at a young age to promote her status and family wealth. Yet it wasn't difficult for Florentino to fall in love with her beauty and grace. She was happy and cherished Cinderella and her servants until she died of the spreading sickness.

"Father"
(Florentino Ozuna/Cinderella's Father)

Looks: age 40; long and dark brown hair; bright emerald green eyes; dark brown skin.
Florentino was a tall and very in shape gentleman due to his many explorations.

Personality: Although Florentino was a kind a generous man he was particular and prudish with an "iron-fist". He expected nothing less from Cinderella than to be a well-educated, elegant young lady.

Background: As a young man, he was bored of the upper class and suggested lifestyle and craved adventure. After meeting Sir Alexander Smith he used his Family's wealth to start their treasure explorations. However, after 20 years of acquiring hard earned riches, he values his family's morals and status enforcing them on Cinderella.

"Ann"
("Sweet Ann"/Elder Stepsister)

Looks: age 18; long, straight and blond hair; fair skin; blue eyes. She was very tall, slender and beautiful.

Personality: The virtuous Ann was truly gentle and graceful in nature. She was quiet, kind and humble.
She was no half-wit but innocent to the lies and darkness

beneath her world.

Background: Ann being the elder sister, and most beautiful, was always paraded by her mother. Humble and naive of her mother's true nature Ann knew that her mother meant well but secretly
desired true love.

"Jezella"
(Younger Stepsister / Minion)

Looks: age 15; curly and dark blonde hair; fair skin; brown eyes.
A little short in height and more curvy than her slender mother and sister. She was more cute then beautiful.

Personality: Jezella was indeed a halfwit. She did not have much common sense and was just as "Dingy" as they come. Yet, Jezella was definitely more modern and open to things more than her family.

Background: She was always "overlooked" by her mother while things focused on Ann. Jezella was eager for a "modern and understanding" role model to follow around. She longed for "attention" as well.

"Stepmother"
(The Duchess of Frey / Cinderella's Stepmother / Arch enemy)

Looks: age 37; brown eyes; very fair skin.
She was very tall and slender like her daughter Ann but with long, straight black hair.

Personality: The duchess was very proper and polite (she was a Lady after all). She was just as much concerned of status and appearances as Frella. She is "smartly silent" until need be. She is a loving mother but truly wicked in nature. Her personality goes from "Lady of honor" to wicked bitch when she feels threatened.

Background: Stepmother was born into wealth and was happy with her 2 daughters until the day her husband died. After losing the love of her life, she learned she had to be scandalous to survive. She learned she had to be wicked when needed. She then turned all her focus on her elder daughter Ann and wanted to ensure they had status and wealth.

"William"
(The Cinderboy and Cinderella's scandalous true Love)

Looks: age 15; long, unstyled and blond hair; dark green eyes; "sun kissed" bronze skin.
He was very tall and slender. He had big, sexy, soft lips and is absolutely delicious!

Personality: Seductive more than anything, William was actually very well spoken and educated (for Cinderella had taught him). He was bold "regardless of status". He could be wicked but his heart is not dark like Cinderella's and he frowns upon being evil or cruel.

Background: William seduced Cinderella at the tender age of 13 and was quite endowed for his age (to say the least). After that, Cinderella was just as wrapped up in William as he was her. They were binded to each other with a love that was more than love. Their original plan was to take over Father's explorations once he passed, get married and live happily ever after.

"Prince Alonso Urena"
(The Prince of Spain / Cinderella's Future Husband)

Looks: age 17; dark brown, styled hair; brown eyes; brown skin.
Tall, very muscular and built. He is most gorgeous!

Personality: Above all very proper. He is young and easily influenced. Eager to escape his guards, is most willing to "sneak off" with Cinderella.

Background: Prince Alonso was raised in a typical Palace setting. His father and royal advisors always did all the "political thinking" for him...until he met Frella. Thinking of her as the boldest and most wise of all women, since his mother died, he truly falls deep for her.

"King Antonio Urena"
(The King of Spain / Alonso's Father)

Looks: age 37; dark brown, styled hair; brown eyes; brown skin.
Tall and very well built like his son...a good looking and seasoned King.

Personality: Above all proper, yet a complete smart ass and very outspoken (when it comes to ruling his Kingdom). However, he is a widower and not too close with his son. He is easily charmed and influenced by Cinderella as well.

Background: The King was raised to care for his people and Kingdom above all. After his wife died he became distant from his son Alonso; focusing constantly on ways to advance his Kingdom.

"King Albert Bloodaxe"
(King of Norway)

Looks: age 45; gray, curly, slightly bald hair; green eyes; fair skin.
He is average in height and extremely fat with a beard.

Personality: He actually has a very jolly personality. He is old fashioned on many things yet open to new ideas. Barbaric in nature and not used to an "intelligent" woman is most intrigued by Cinderella. He, of course, lusts for her quietly as well.

Background: Unlike the King of Spain, King Albert was not born into Royalty, he had to fight for it. In the Northerners culture they made their best warrior King. King Albert led many successful battles, had a happy reign and was easily seduced by a woman. Having no male heirs, King Albert made the decision to be more political and advanced in his old age.

"Stable Boy #1"
(Drake Penya / Minion)

Looks: age 19; long, unstyled, brown hair; green eyes; brown skin.
Tall and slender built and very sexy like William.

Personality: He has a very serious personality. No humor or joy (like a British guard). He only lives for his work including his many...many side jobs serving Cinderella.

Background: After both parents died (whom were loyal servants of her parents), Cinderella's kind hearted mother kept Drake and his younger brother Alejandro; giving them food, shelter, and pay for taking care of the horses. Drake had always been secretly in love with Frella, doing any...and every wicked task she ask. So dedicated to her, for she was "his" Queen, he'd lay down his life for her. Putting Cinderella on the highest of pedestals, he was too shy to admit his feelings for her before William.

"Stable Boy #2"
(Alejandro Penya / Minion)

Looks: age 17; long, unstyled, brown hair; brown eyes; brown skin.
He is also tall and slender built (like his brother) and very sexy.

Personality: He is kind of…Jezella's male counterpart. He is young, easily influenced and not so bright. He simply follows his older brother Drake around, stays quiet, and does what he is told.

Background: After his parents died of the spreading sickness, Cinderella's kind mother took him and his older brother Drake in; giving them food, shelter and payment in return for taking care of the horses. Alejandro knows nothing else than to be a stable boy and loyal to his employer.

"Sir Fredrick Henhsaw"
(Neighboring Nobel/Father's Friend)

Looks: age 44; gray hair; brown eyes; brown skin.
He is average in height and very built and in shape for his age. (Handsome for an old brute.)

Personality: He is the wealthiest Nobel next to Cinderella's father. Very snooty, "proper" in tone and a (know it all). Although he is polite, he boasts of himself and accomplishments to flirt.

Background: His wife has been gone many years while giving birth to his son who didn't live either. She was friend with Cinderella's mother. So, instead of grieving, Sir Fredrick prides himself on his wealth and many…many scandalous affairs.

"Sir Alexander Smith"

Looks: age 45; gray hair; brown eyes; brown skin.
He was a very tall and very husky gentleman.

Personality: Sir Alexander Smith was the kindest man you could ever meet. He was more than focused on his life's work and explorations (always chasing a new discovery and treasure). Although he was a very proper and concentrated man…he would give you his gold and the shirt off his back.

Background: His friendship with Cinderella's father started nearly 20 years ago. He sort of looked at Florentino as a younger brother and promised to "always take care of him" during their first treasure hunt. He never married or had children and always looked at Cinderella like a daughter.

CHAPTER I

"INTRODUCTIONS"

Once upon a time there was a young Nobel named Frella. But her servants all called her Cinderella behind her back...due to the fact she was having an affair with her Cinderboy. She was a sinister and vengeful girl. She was truly wicked! How the story got twisted into making her stepmother and stepsisters evil I'll never understand. But, let's start from the beginning shall we.

Cinderella was a happy child growing up. Her Father and Mother were good and honorable Nobles. Everything was as it should be until the day her mother died from the spreading sickness. At the tender age of 12 Cinderella turned dark. Her grieving heart for her mother, the beautiful light and inspiration of her life, is what stared this wicked story. One of manipulation, murder, seduction and most of all...a lust for power to try to fill the hole of her empty black heart.

She loved her father as well, of course. She was just never very close with him being constantly away searching for treasure. He much up kept his mansion, servants, and darling daughter in style. In fact, once her mother was gone, she preferred for her father to be away. That way she could run the household as she pleased. She could be her evil self while pretending to be a Nobel Lady of honor in public...and especially a sweet girl while daddy was around. But the day he brought her stepmother and two beautiful stepsisters home...that was the day she truly became...evil! Enraged with jealously over her elder stepsister's beauty and fear her stepmother would take over her power, she came up with a plan to make them suffer and rule the house that was rightfully hers. But having this completion made her realize, in order to truly rule and make others sarcomere to your will, she had to rule the Kingdom as well. But, first things first. Let's start with these annoying little stepsisters shall we.

The first thing Cinderella thought when Jezella stepped out of the carriage was, "Wow, this little twit will be easy to turn into my minion." However, when Ann stepped out Cinderella knew at first glance she was not only gorgeous but kind as well as wise. She knew she had work to do. And last but not least, when she saw her new stepmother step out of that carriage, it took everything she had not to rip that bitch's throat out at first sight! For she knew "Stepmother" could destroy everything. A true champion knows a worthy opponent. Cinderella was more than excellent in the game of chess, on the board as well as in life. Her and her mother always played leaving Cinderella almost now obsessed with playing life like the game. And when Stepmother stepped out of that carriage...the future Queen knew she had met her match!

"Hello Stepmother. Welcome to our lovely home. I'm Frella," said dear Cinderella in the sweetest tone.

"Lovely to meet you dear. May I introduce my two daughters? My eldest Ann and her sister Jezella," said Stepmother.

The two girls seemed happy to be there and intrigued by their new stepsister. And Cinderella thought to herself while she had to secure her place as Lady of the House... She might actually have fun with these two tarts!

She looked at Stepmother and replied, "I suppose Father couldn't be here as usual."

Stepmother responded, "Yes, dear. I am sorry but this will give us a better chance to bond, just us girls."

Cinderella immediately made it clear Stepmother would NOT be taking over. In which she replied, "Yes. I'll be happy to show you how things are ran in MY house," as she smiled sarcastically. At this point Stepmother was silent, thinking to herself this snotty 17 year old little girl couldn't possibly be a threat. "The servants here are loyal and obedient. You see they are the best paid in all the land," said Cinderella. Stepmother just nodded and replied, "I see," as she followed Cinderella upstairs (her daughters close behind). Cinderella wasn't sure if the stepsisters were silent out of fear or curiosity. She could all but hope it was fear and intended to keep it that way.

Her servants feared for their life and that of their families if they told about her laying with her Cinderboy at night. She had to make an example of one servant girl by poisoning the girl's father with fancy wine as a "reward for his daughter's promotion". She then buried the girl only up to her head as she slowly poisoned her for three days. The other servants needed to know the price for disloyalty. But Cinderella was smarter than your usual male tyrant. She understood someone would fight for you out of fear...yet die for you out of loyalty. On the third day while the two stable boys buried the rest of the girl Cinderella gathered all her servants around and rewarded them with rubies. She explained she loved the servants shed grown up with. She shed a few tears as she said how she couldn't understand how the servant girl would threatened her so. She couldn't understand why she would try to ruin their happy life for her being truly in love with her Cinderboy. Cinderella made it perfectly clear you would pay for your betrayal, however, be handsomely rewarded for your loyalty.

She said to her servants, "This is a house of many secrets. Yet let there be none between this family... anything you ever need of me just ask." Cinderella couldn't help but think of this day while she show her new stepfamily "The Intruders" her home.

"Let me show you the lovely garden where my mother showed me how to grow many lovely flowers," she said to Stepmother.

"That's lovely dear," replied Stepmother, having no idea Cinderella used it for growing and brewing many lovely poisons as well. I'm sure that was not her mother's intent while teaching Frella to garden, but this was before she died, leaving Cinderella alone with her pain. As Cinderella thought of this pain, she quickly realized she had no time to waste. She then informed her Stepmother she would show them to their quarters. As she did so, she informed them the ENTIRE third floor was hers. Stepmother was curious as she asked, "the attic?" Cinderella smiled and replied, "My quarters are the largest and finest in the house I assure you." As she sweetly smiled she knew the attic was the best place for secret passages among other things.

She also knew to strike the weakest link first. Therefore, she saved Jezella's room for last so she could get started on seducing her new informant/lap dog. As she seductively brushed Jezella's shoulder, she told Jezella she had saved the prettiest room for the prettiest sister.

"I've always wanted a sister," said Cinderella. "I get lonely here. May I come in?" Jezella seemed happy to invite Cinderella in. Being the youngest and most naive, she was always "overlooked" by her mother and elder sister. Cinderella somehow knew that and was going to use to manipulate Jezella.

"So, what is it like being the youngest? I bet everything focuses on you," said Cinderella. In which her stepsister shyly responded, "Actually everything is always focused on Ann. She is the eldest and more pretty than I." Cinderella quickly replied, "Well that's not fair, is it? And you're so beautiful, I bet she's just jealous. Don't worry, this is my house and I will make sure my darling new little sister gets all the respect she deserves. We are going to be great friends!" She could see this sort of compliment was rare to Jezella and lifted her spirits. Jezella smile sincerely at Cinderella as she left the room. Cinderella smiled back, for she was genuinely happy at this moment knowing this would be all too easy. One down...two to go!

"Now what am I supposed to do with this next stepsister of mine," Cinderella thought to herself. "She is no halfwit. She obviously is no ally neither, she is far too kind, it would be difficult to change that and I have a wicked Stepmother to worry about." Cinderella mumbled to herself as she walked towards her attic (where she no doubtable planned on meeting her Cinderboy in their secret quarters). Cinderella had many secret passages built all through the house so she could keep an eye on everyone along with a secret room. It was a tad small for her refined taste. But, it was a disguised a thick wall triggered by Cinderella's favorite art piece.

Of course an intelligent lady such as she had a taste for the arts and sciences. Besides, she cared not where she lay with her Cinderboy, as long as she was with William.

Her body was binded to that of William's. His long slender fingers, she couldn't wait for them to touch her. His deep dark green eyes made her melt. His long, unstyled, blonde hair, his tall perfect body... She thought everything about him was beautiful. And when his soft lips touched hers, she couldn't wait for him to be inside her. She loved him so. Yes, it was difficult to think of anything else while William was around...but even he could not change her dark heart.

CHAPTER II

"THE PARTY"

A girl with no mother and an absent father learned young; when playing chess...you must manipulate to win! Cinderella would let nothing get in the way of her happiness. She felt she did not deserve to lose her mother, therefore, EVERYONE deserved to feel her wrath. "There's no way I'm going to let these three horrid little whores take over my home. It is my mansion NOT theirs! All I have left is my father, my servants, my family and...my love. Nothing will ever keep me from him. This wicked stepfamily must learn their lesson." Cinderella thought to herself as she smiled across the breakfast table.

"So Stepmother, I was thinking how lovely it would be to introduce my wonderful new family to society. I know your just getting settled. But, perhaps when Father returns we can have a little party! Not only to celebrate his return, but to announce your arrival as well. What do you think?" Cinderella said. Jezella was all but too excited. Ann was more humble about the party but excited about the idea. Stepmother knew it would not be wise to decline and was just as concerned about appearances as Frella. She politely responded, "Of course dear, how lovely." Cinderella could see right through that ridiculous "false" smile. But she was more than happy to begin this battle.

Cinderella being wise far beyond her years knew; the best way to see someone's truth, and weakness, is to see them drunk. She laughed to herself as she thought of this. "And of course under the pressures of society" Cinderella smiled sweetly as she thought of all the wicked plans she could conspire with a simple get together of: her friends, "the intruders" and good wine.

"I'm not sure what to do with this kind stepsister yet. But I can certainly show Father what a whore and gold digger this new wife of his really is. Then he'll see she is not fit to rule this house." Cinderella was jolly as she thought of this…Sir Fredrick Henshaw came to mind. He was the Lord of the largest sheep farm in the land. Perverted as he was handsome, for an old brute, Cinderella knew he was perfect to plant thoughts into Father's head. "All I need to do first is plant the seed in Sir Fredrick's head," she thought. "Then I shall introduce him to Stepmother as I plant thoughts of 'impure intentions' to Father from afar. Jezella shall come in handy." Weeks past as Cinderella plot her wicked soiree'. Father was about to return as Cinderella drew closer to Jezella. Making sure Jezella realized "she" was the one to follow… The one who cared, the one who could help her shine as she deserved to (more than her family thought). Stepmother bided her time continuing her love/hate relationship with her stepdaughter. She not yet interfere with Cinderella running the mansion. Cinderella rarely spoke to her elder stepsister, for she knew she had to knock out the Queen before worrying about a pond.

Cinderella knew right before the party was the time to have a "casual chat" with Jezella about her part in this plan. She also knew to tell William to keep his distance when father returned. William did whatever Cinderella asked. He knew how evil she could be…but loved her still.

"Jezella," said Cinderella, "is my favorite and most gorgeous stepsister nervous about the party tonight?"

"Quite the opposite sister," stated Jezella.

"And why should you be? You'll be the fairest there. I'm sure your mother, however, is most uneasy."

"Why do you say that?" Jezella asked. Cinderella smiled.

"You see my dear, Sir Fredrick Henshaw is the Lord of the largest sheep farm in all the land. My father has been wanting him to invest in his explorations for years. Oh! But, please do not mention that to daddy, he might be embarrassed. Your mother should meet him though, set her mark in society! It would be a grand union if he were to 'invest'. Being married to my father and meeting our friends well…she must be exceedingly charming. If my father were to hear of her persuading Sir Fredrick to invest, he'd be most pleased. Perhaps… You could boast to him! I'll speak with stepmother and make the introduction," stated Cinderella.

Cinderella was glad of her father's return. But, she was all too happy to put Stepmother in her place. Moments before Stepmother entered the party, Cinderella was sure to put the pressure on.

"Stepmother…you are such a beauty to behold," said Cinderella kindly.

"Why thank you dear," Stepmother replied.

"Oh and Stepmother… All the Lords and 'investors' are here. Between you and I, they will be all too happy and willing to invest in our new family. One Lady to another." Cinderella spoke ever so sweet. She then quickly changed tone from requesting to demanding firmly and said, "You are expected to be more than charming to our friends. Understand?" as she entered the party.

She made many introductions. She was known as the most humble and fairest of all Nobles, always caring for others. However, she couldn't help but notice all the eyes on her elder stepsister Ann. This much enraged Cinderella. She knew she must quickly enact Stepmother's downfall so she could soon deal with Sweet Ann. She rushed to her newest lap dog/stepsister and made sure to send her Father's way. Then she carefully and seductively approached Sir Fredrick.

"Sir Frederick Henshaw, lovely to see you again!" said Cinderella.

"And you are dazzling as usual Frella," said Sire Fredrick.

"Why thank you Sir," Cinderella said kindly as she stepped closer to his ear. "My stepmother is gorgeous isn't she? She is much lonely while Father's away. I no doubt believe she is far more 'modern' than she leads on. I think she's dying on the inside...for a little fun." She seductively whispered. And guess who happened to be walking by that very moment.

"Oh Stepmother," Cinderella spoke loudly enough so Stepmother could not ignore. Her stepmother politely nodded. "This is Sir Fredrick Henshaw, Lord of the most prestigious sheep farm in all the land. Sir Fredrick this is my beautiful stepmother The Duchess of Frey. She is more than happy to attend this soiree' and make new...friends. I'll let the two of you get better acquainted." Cinderella said politely as she scallied away to check on Father.

Cinderella was all too happy to see her stupid stepsister speaking to Father. She let them speak. And as soon as she seen his surprised and NOT so pleased face turn, she quickly interrupted.

"Pardon me Jezella, may I have a moment with my father please," said Cinderella politely.

"Of course dear sister," Jezella said quietly as she quietly dismissed herself.

"So, Father, how is our new family blending in?" Cinderella asked Father.

As he couldn't help but notice Sir Frederick's flirtations… He also noticed his wife was not dismissing them. "It seems the Duchess is eager to acquire investors. Frella do you know anything about his?" proclaimed Father.

"Of course not." Cinderella said innocently. "Why would she feel a need to expand our wonderful estate? Perhaps it's not enough for her. Then again, she is lonely here. Maybe she just wants some new friends." Cinderella stated as she acted oblivious to the world around her. "Father, I wouldn't mention anything just yet if I were you" she said assertively as her father nodded and continued to watch the two.

— *C.H.Darkling* —

CHAPTER III

"LEGALITIES AND FUN"

The next morning Cinderella was all but too eager to make it crystal clear to her father that Stepmother was no way fir to run their house (if she hadn't already done so last night). But when she entered Father's business quarters, Cinderella was surprised to see Father was already up and involved in pressing matters.

"Father I wanted to speak with you about Stepmother." Cinderella said swiftly. Her father, giving her, giving her no time to continue immediately responded, "I have no concern with that at the moment. Our funds of precious jewels is lower than usual. It would seem we have a thief in our mists!" (Cinderella had been skimming a part of each treasure discovery for years, hiding them in a secret chest that even William was unaware of.) However, she was not about to let on her guilt now. She acted most surprised and deeply concerned as she responded, "Father, how long do you think this has been happening?"

Cinderella knew she could quickly blame "the intruders" if recent. "More coal to my fire" she thought. However, if Father suspected this decrease in funds happened over time...she knew she had to blame a servant. Cinderella was not happy of this as she loved her servants but would do ANYTHING to protect William. How lucky for our Evil Cinder... Father responded, "This disloyalty must have happened recently." Cinderella was raving with joy on the inside! She was delighted to have all the more reason to stomp "Father's new whore" further into the ground. However, this chess player knew she must sound more upset than angry to be more believable.

Cinderella quickly responded, "That's what I wanted to talk to you about Father." Father was all too curious...and angered. He immediately dismissed all servants. Once they closed the door, Cinderella immediately said, "I've been thinking about what you mentioned last night about Stepmother being eager to expand? (Rhetorical question) Well, you know me. I'm always the first to think the best of someone. But Stepmother has been spending a lot of rubies lately and always making sure the stepsister's are in the latest fashions. I thought nothing of it at first. I'm so glad to see my two sisters, I've always longed for, happy. Are you sure someone so eager to squander your hard earned riches can be trusted?"

Father paused. Therefore Cinderella was quick to reply, "Father...this mansion and our wonderful and most loyal servants are all we have left of Mother." Cinderella shed a few tears while saying this. Then she quickly changed to a serious note and said, "I think you should send word for our family lawyer and make ME legal Lady of the House, as your only blood daughter that is. Just until we know whom to trust, alright Father?"

Her father nodded in agreement. Cinderella left the room and headed towards her lovely poison garden. She often would go out her to collect strategy. She smiled as she had a sense of serenity. And as she thought, "Two down...one to go," she whispered to herself, "now I deserve a little fun."

"What to do, what to do with this kind stepsister of mine..." Cinderella began to think. "She's far too good to think ill of my intentions. Yet, she's far too wise for simple manipulation. So, how can I humiliate someone of her grace for my amusement?" Cinderella uttered to herself. But then she remembered a rare mandrake root that if eaten, would make you go deaf for three days. Cinderella knew this was a trivial trick in all reality but it would give her a good laugh never-the-less. She had, of course, sent her stable boy to fetch it from the neighboring land before. Therefore, Cinderella laughed as she plot a very special dessert for that evening.

As Lady of the House, it was not unusual to request a dessert of her desire. It was also not rare for William to tease Cinderella in the cooking quarters, in the lower level of the mansion. He would often sweep the cinders down there whilst Cinderella acted extremely interested in watching the servants cook. Cinderella always pretended to be pestered by William getting her fine dresses dirty. However, when William ran his dirty cinder hands up her skirt, then onto her thighs, she loved it. Cinderella felt as if she was melting into a puddle.

As Cinderella was requesting blackberry cobbler, which blended perfectly with mandrake root, William surprised her with his long sexy arms around her waist.

"Waiting for me my love?" said William.

"Ugh, William!" Cinderella squealed. "Believe it or not, I'm actually learning how to make blackberry cobbler." Cinderella replied. She could not let William know she was being cruel for fun. She led him to believe she was indeed there waiting on him and not her stable boy. So when he pushed her up against a wall and kissed her aggressively, with passion, she could not help but to give in. But even he could not distract her from her wicked ways. As soon as she saw her stable boy in the distance, she knew she had to dismiss William.

"William what are you doing!" Cinderella giggled. "There are new threats to our happiness, remember?" she asked.

"Your snobby stepfamily will never come down here," said William.

"Never-the-less my darling, I do not trust my wicked stepmother and stepsisters. I feel her eyes upon me lately. If you but please meet me in the attic tonight! We can fuck like animals once Father leaves." Cinderella informed him. William nodded as he left and kissed her once more. Cinderella's dark hear was warmed... As she seen her stable boy draw closer with her mandrake root. She added it generously in a separate cobbler in a small pan. She told her servant the small pan was for Ann's plate ONLY. "This does not leave this room, understand?" Cinderella said as she left to bid her father farewell.

Cinderella was almost as happy as she was before her wicked stepfamily arrived. She pleasantly jaunted to say goodbye to Father and remind him to send for a secret meeting with the family lawyer. She couldn't wait to tell her father "he'd made the right decision to be wary of Stepmother" nor to see Sweet Ann take that first bite! However, Cinderella knew she must contain her emotions and present herself properly to see Father off. Afterwards, she ordered the servants to prepare for dinner. She then summoned her maids and asked to be dressed in a very special dress...for a very special evening.

Cinderella looked more than elegant for a quiet family dinner. You could see her glowing from a distances she glided down the stairs. She was eager to be seated and begin some pleasant dinner conversation.

"So Stepmother, I saw you speaking with Sir Fredrick Henshaw for a while. I do hope you think he was charming. He would be a grand merger for us. Don't you think?" said Cinderella.

Stepmother being the wicked cow she is seemed interested in the merger. Yet she responded, "I'm still settling in dear. I'm not certain of any investors at the moment. Sir Fredrick seems to be an 'aggressive' gentleman."

Cinderella couldn't help but chuckle a little as she replied, "He is, but it is all in good jest I assure you. He *is* a most necessary asset to our reputation here Stepmother." Stepmother just smiled politely.

Cinderella also took it upon herself to announce the blackberry cobbler was an old recipe of her mother's. "You all must try it!" Cinderella said enthusiastically as she glanced at her elder stepsister. "The local bakery even sells it at the town square. Everyone says it's most delicious!" said Cinderella. Jezella, of course, was intrigued by Frella's every word as she responded, "How wonderful, I'm sure it will be the best dessert I've ever had!"

Stepmother smirked in silence. And the more refined Ann politely replied, "Of course sister, I'm sure it's lovely." "Lovely indeed," Cinderella thought as she watched Sweet Ann take a bite of her "lovely" tainted cobbler! Cinderella just smiled softly, with deceitful wiles, as she imagined laughing incessantly the next morning, when Sweet Ann awoke and realized she was deprived of her hearing.

CHAPTER IV

"THE DEATH"

The next morning Cinderella stayed in her attic. She knew her secret quarters would come in handy as she waited the chaos. She sit patiently reading of politics and poetry until she heard the sweet screams and shrieks of her wicked stepfamily. She knew she must contain her joy. As she hear rapid footsteps up the stairs, Jezella hectically barged into her quarters yelling, "It's Ann! She's gone deaf! What could we have possibly done to deserve this?! Oh, the world's coming to an end!" Cinderella acted stunned and much concerned as she tried to calm her minion. She assured Jezella she would ready the carriage immediately for a trip to the medic at the town square.

As Cinderella hurry down the stairs to witness the wonderful catastrophe she had caused, she saw servants scattering and Stepmother in a state of frenzy. She could not help but to smirk quickly before approaching her.

"Stepmother there is no time for a house call! The carriage is prepared. You must get Ann to the medic immediately! Perhaps there is an explanation for her loss of hearing." Cinderella said in all seriousness.

"Where is she?!" Stepmother yelled as she scurried about like a chicken with no head. Cinderella was more than pleased with herself to find Ann in the corner of the dining area crying her pretty little eyes out.

As her wicked stepfamily enter the carriage, Cinderella reassured them everything would be alright once they arrived at the local medics. Knowing the local medic would have no knowledge of the mandrake root, nor its affects, Cinderella rushed upstairs to enjoy herself. She laughed uncontrollably for a while in her secret quarters. She imagined the grief, the worry and the humiliation of torturing her stepsister. She then started to giggle hysterically, almost, thinking of the distress they would have…only to be fine as wine in three days' time. Cinderella was exceedingly happy when she thought of this! If only she knew her happiness was not to last.

Cinderella much enjoyed the next few days. Watching Stepmother yell more and more loudly at Ann (as though it would make her hear) was most hilarious. Cinderella laughed only on the inside thinking, "Perhaps this whore really *is* a half-wit after all." Yes, the Lady of the house was having a splendid time making Sweet Ann suffer. That is, until a messenger arrived at the front door with an urgent letter. It took Cinderella no time snatching it from his hand (assuming it was word from her family lawyer) since it was addressed to Lady of the House. Cinderella's heart suddenly dropped to the pit of her stomach after what she read next.

> *Dear Frella,*
>
> *Your father has fallen ill due to the spreading sickness in our recent expedition. I have already sent for the best of medics to your home. I will watch over him as I promised years ago. We are traveling as swift as possible. We will arrive in two weeks' time so we can better care for him. I'm so sorry.*
>
> *Smith*

Sir Alexander Smith had been a loyal employee of

father's for as long as she could remember. She knew his loyalty and that he would take care of Father as promised. However, Cinderella worried that even modern advances in medicine (since the sickness took her mother) would not be enough. "There's no way in hell I'm going to let the only TRUE family I have be taken from me...not again!" Cinderella uttered to herself. She nearly fell to the floor with despair but she quickly arose for she had not time to waste to save her father.

Cinderella quickly alerted her Stepmother of the message. "I am truly sorry my dear. This is most devastating news," replied Stepmother (as if she actually cared). Cinderella was quick to interrupt her apologies as well.

"This is no time for your nonsense. I do say Madame, your inability to control your emotions did poor Ann no good...as her loss of hearing was only temporary. There is NOTHING to be sorry about Stepmother. We have already sent for the best of all medics and must IMMEDIATELY prepare for Father's recovery. On this matter tis nonnegotiable." said Cinderella more than forcefully. Stepmother was sincerely speechless. She nodded in agreement but not to be polite. But, in that brief moment, she actually felt sorry for the poor girl.

Stepmother began to think, as Cinderella whisked away, "What if he die? How will we live? How much trust funds do we have? And perhaps we should have merged with that ghastly Sir Fredrick. The medics could save him...but what if they cannot?" Stepmother then came to a conclusion: she must prepare for her husband's recovery, yet make other preparations as well. "If I can convince this snobby and spiteful little girl to marry a Duke, perhaps, before *my* daughters...it would ensure our survival." Stepmother thought to herself.

For the next two weeks Cinderella kept busy preparing for her father's return. She made time not for toying with stepsisters and hardly not even William (for she was much too tired by nightfall). Her stepmother spent this time trying to falsely bond with Cinderella. Stepmother, having malicious intentions, did her best to put Cinderella under her wing. The Duchess knew that Frella would be essential to her status...in one way or another. She planned on putting their new bond to use for some "motherly manipulation".

It was time for Father to arrive. The anticipation caused Cinderella to become more "unbalanced" than she already was. She trusted not her and her stepmother's newfound relationship, but was only concerned with nursing Father back to health. She was actually in this moment truly happy for his return (as she had not been for years). Cinderella was regretful of lost time with Father but was more than excited to make it up to him. As the carriage became closer and closer to the mansion, Cinderella said to herself, "Don't worry Father. I have the means to save you this time...not like Mother. I won't leave your side!"

As her stepfamily await patiently inside, Cinderella's heart filled with joy as she seen Sir Smith get out of the carriage! However, his face implied he was not happy to see her... He beheld both her hands, he look down, he spoke not and shake his head no. Cinderella fell into his arms as she burst into uncontrollable tears! She contained herself not. She was in too much of a state of shock and overwhelming sadness. Too distraught from another *unfair* death... Cinderella think not of legalities.

CHAPTER V

"THE HOSTILE TAKEOVER"

The death of Cinderella's father was tragic indeed. But Stepmother, of course, could always be counted upon to have ambition and status on her mind. Poor Cinderella, overcome by grief, was inconsolable for weeks. She did not even attend her father's funeral. She could not bare the thought of burying him. As she wallow in her sorrows...her stepmother did NOT hesitate to take over the duties of "Lady of the House". She order the servants about. She waltz through the mansion as if she were Queen. And, with her husband's passing, she became much more outspoken. Stepmother's true colors were showing day by day. Cinderella enclosed in her attic notice not for she had even told her maids to order her Cinderboy away. Jezella, of course, made attempts to comfort her but Cinderella wanted to be left alone...until one day her servants drew her a bath.

As Cinderella lay in the tub, she try to relax her aching heart and wash away her tears. She then, to her surprise, felt the long and slender fingers of...

"William!" Cinderella shrieked. "William, what are you doing? Can't you see I'm no use to you at the moment! Can't you see I'm distressed?" she sighed. As he gazed upon her with his deep, dark green eyes, his hands rub her so seductively furtherer down her body. As his sweet soft lips get closer to hers, Cinderella could never deny him.

"The only use I have for you, or need, is your love my darling." William whispered sweetly as he kiss her neck. Cinderella realized that she'd missed his touch, then realized, she needed it. Cinderella then aggressively pulled him into the bath with her as he began to kiss her forcefully with passion.

But as I said before, even William could not change her dark heart; especially with her father now gone. Cinderella did give into passion. However, when William asked her to leave her quarters and go on a midnight stroll, like they used to, she declined. When she did so, he proceeded to inform her of Stepmother running the house.

"My love, are you really going to let that snobby witch take over our home?!" William proclaimed.

"What! What do you mean?" Cinderella asked intently.

"She comes forth to order us about. The lady is much more verbal now to say the least. And, I saw her talking to Sir Fredrick at your father's burial. It looked most suspicious my love," William stated.

Cinderella arose and covered herself quickly. "The nerve of that wench! She dare converse with my father's associate when I turn my back! What treacheries is she up to?! My father lay in the found and she attempt to act like a Lady? This whore has mistaken me for a sweet country girl." Cinderella shout. It was then she awaken from her despair…for battle had been brought! Outraged by Stepmother's actions, Cinderella then lock her grief in her dark, heart shaped box (only William has the key). She looked at him and reply, "No…for *I* am Lady of this house!"

Cinderella then summoned for a maid to dress her, for she indeed was going on a midnight stroll. William then held out his hand for hers as they proceeded through a secret corridor leading to the back vineyard. Cinderella was already acting like her old self as she plot many ways to put Stepmother in her place, most regally and legally.

"So my darling, tell me more of Stepmother and your suspicions" said Cinderella.

"Well she truly is turning into a wicked stepmother indeed my love. I thought you were just being cynical as usual. But she belittled your maid Mary yesterday, Oh! Over a sash! And she then pay us with a few gold coins!" William said in anger.

She did not like to see her Cinderboy upset nor her loving servants treated like dogs. Cinderella grew angrier of this. She knew to keep a happy servant loyal, you must show them appreciation. She preferred to have her "small army" (as she liked to call them) follow her out of loyalty more than fear. She then wanted to know more of Stepmother and Sir Fredrick's conversation.

"I'm not certain my love. But they looked to be having a more than long chat of something of a serious matter! It felt as if they were in league" said William.

"I don't know what that harolette is conspiring but if she makes any efforts to take what is mine by marrying him... He WILL fall to an untimely death!" replied Cinderella in all seriousness.

"FRELLA!" William shout. "You know I do not like for you to be cruel!" He snarled at her.

"As I have explained before William, sometimes you have to be cruel...to be kind. Sometimes I must be forced to be wicked, evil even. I take no pleasure in this my darling (as she shed a glistening tear). But, certain acts MUST be punished accordingly. Its justice! And it is my job as a Nobel Lady and ruler of this house to protect you, to protect *us* and our happiness. Is it not?!" Cinderella stated firmly.

"Yes my love. Forgive me. I would smite whom I need, if he dare stand in front of me...to get to you." William said ever so lovingly. He then grab Cinderella's waist and pulled her body close, forcefully, but gentle and kissed her. Cinderella indulged in his sweet soft lips as everything disappeared for a brief moment. She then run her fingers through his long, unstyled, blond messy hair (that she loved) and gasped.

"William! You must immediately send the stable boy to message my family lawyer. Please! There is no time to waste!" she shout. William obeyed quickly as Cinderella return to her quarters, for she had a lot to do tomorrow.

The next morning as Cinderella awoke, she summoned for her maids to "dress her stylishly". As she gazed upon herself in the mirror, she think out loud, "Let the battles begin Stepmother... I'm rather looking forward to it." This time around she had no intention of playing coy when it came to informing Stepmother whom "Lady of this mansion" was. Cinderella hurried down the stairs. She wanted to make sure the servants knew who they would be taking orders from before Stepmother slithered her way in. As Stepmother enter the dining area for breakfast, she was all but too surprised to see "Frella" sitting at the breakfast table (next to Jezella of course). Cinderella was *thanking* her "helping her realize she still had family". Stepmother was expecting to see a "broken" and "discouraged" young girl, not a civil young lady. Never-the-less, Stepmother considered her no threat.

"Frella, I am happy to see you eating. Us girls have got to stick together now more than ever," said Stepmother casually.

"Of course Stepmother I most certainly appreciate you taking me under your wing and especially for tending to the mansion…in my absence." Stepmother thinking Cinderella *naïve* replied, "My dear I do not want you to worry about business matters. I am your mother now. I will take care of things. I will see you no more under further distress." Oops! Stepmother just said the WRONG thing.

"You! Are NOT my mother Duchess. *I* am the blood heiress and Lady of this House. I am most pleased to have this family here with Father's passing. But perhaps *you* shouldn't worry your uneducated head about this mansion and our business matters." Cinderella stated with force and much displeasure. As Stepmother opened her mouth to speak Cinderella immediately interrupted her with a demeaning manor, "Thank you for your concern. But I am in position to take over my obligations." So Stepmother replied, "My dear I am a Nobel's widow. You are but a 17 year old child whom has unfairly been put in this position. Legally *I* am the rightful heir. And, have you even considered our survival once the precious jewels run out in your 'unsteady state'?

Cinderella then replied, "I believe I've lost my appetite. But just to be clear, Stepmother, I am familiar with the investors and this Society more than *You*! For starters our servant's salary is a bit more than a few gold coins. One of us…MUST marry. If we but merger with investors perhaps hiring another employee to continue my father's explorations with Sir Smith…we should actually do quite well for ourselves. So you see… I am NO child. And by the way Stepmother, my family lawyer is riding here this very moment to ensure there are no legal disputes about whom is legally Lady of the house," as she exited the room. Stepmother was left speechless. Ann and Jezella simply starred at each other with no knowledge of these matters or what was to be said.

As Stepmother sit there with her wicked plots of a "hostile takeover" she made preparations of her own. She wondered how Frella knew about the servants payments. "No doubt of them wined like a baby and told you things…little girl!" She thought to herself. She then (after sending an urgent message with a garden tenant) made her way to the family office where Cinderella and her lawyer were indeed awaiting her.

When the Duchess enter the room, she overheard the family lawyer telling Cinderella "he had received no such message". Stepmother was pleased of this for she had her own "arrangements". However, the lawyer also stated if Frella could find *any* documentation "with her father's signature making her legal Lady of the house", it would make all the difference.

"Also my Lady, being this a Nobel's property and not Royalty, it can be disputed legally due to your very young age regardless of you being the only blood heir indeed," stated the lawyer.

At that moment (and not a moment too soon) Sir Fredrick Henshaw announced himself. Cinderella was stunned. Her heart dropped. Stepmother smirked.

"If I may Sir," he rudely interrupted. "As the Widow, the Duchess is indeed the rightful heir unless you have a Will stating otherwise. I have merged my estate with that of the Duchess entitling *me* as Lord of this property as we are to divide the profits. Also, Frella, if you desire, I advise you to marry my younger cousin whom is indeed a wealthy Duke." He stated most properly.

Cinderella was enraged with fury. She restrained herself not as she (with incredible force) literally ran across the office and attempted to strangle her Stepmother. Sir Fredrick and her lawyer both pulled her away and attempted to calm her. She then slapped Sir Fredrick straight across the face. She yelled in anger, "I thought it was Stepmother's intention to marry you, like an imbecile, but this... THIS is betrayal! Both of you!" She snarled at Stepmother as she said this, "You conspire to marry *me* off whilst you waste my father's riches?" She then look at Stepmother and replied, "No... my answer is no. You will NOT dismiss me so easily Stepmother." She was close enough to kiss her stepmother as she said this.

Cinderella then left the room making close eye contact with her betrayer, Sir Fredrick, on her way out. She whispered in his hear "YOU...have yet to feel my wrath," as she passed him. Stepmother dismissed her as a sweet country girl, a child with a snotty attitude and innocent temper. As Cinderella proceeded to her attic she spoke softly to herself, "You have won the battle Stepmother... but NOT the war."

CHAPTER VI

"THE PRINCE"

Cinderella had been mistaken for a sweet, uncomplicated, country girl indeed. However, she was anything but.

It was that very moment Cinderella realized in order to overpower her enemies and truly bend others to her will...she must become royalty! Cinderella was always much too involved with William to ever think of the Prince before. She couldn't help but think he was her age, good-looking, and sure as sheep's shit probably as stupid as any man (when it came to seduction). Cinderella also realized that 17 was "the coming of age" for royalty and she must work quickly if she were to devise a plan. However, if William wasn't the first to hear of this plan...he would be most displeased with her. "How am I to convince him this is for *us*?" She thought. Then it came to her and she summoned her Cinderboy that night.

As William entered their secret quarters, Cinderella walked up to him slowly...seductive. She rubbed both her hands up his chest and to his neck ever so provocative. She then softly kissed the left side of his neck... then the right. She then rubbed her fingers through his long hair (that she loved) and pulled as she aggressively pushed him onto the settee. She screamed (as if being tortured...but *so* good!) as she rode him like a stallion.

"Fuck me my love!" she moaned passionately. "I Love you so much." Cinderella grabbed his face with both hands and then kissed him with force as William pulled her body close to his and brought her rocking hips to a halt. William then sweetly touch Cinderella's face and declared how much he loved her. In which Cinderella replied, "You still wish to marry me then my darling?"

"In my dreams every night my love," said William.

Therefore, Cinderella explained to him the only way she would have the power to entitle him to a station high enough to marry her…she would have to become royalty.

"I know you cannot bare the thought of me marrying another my darling, but you knew this day would come. At least as Queen I could entitle you to a Duke of great lands. Only then, could we truly be together… once I am a widowed Queen." Cinderella said to William intently. Although he was upset, William knew his place as Cinderboy and he argued not. Cinderella then shed one glistening tear and said, "My wicked stepmother has conspired to steal EVERYTHING from us! My ONLY choice is to marry the Prince, if we ever want a chance at a happy life together. I am truly sorry for what I have to do next…but this is ALL my stepmother's doing, William, not mine!" William simply looked down and sighed, "I know."

Over the next few days Cinderella avoided Stepmother by "shopping in the town square". And while in town, by the Palace, she wasted no time using her wicked wiles (and rubies) to bribe the Prince's guards. How lucky for her she found out the Prince would be hunting by a nearby Nobel's farm. Cinderella made sure she was gathering apples by her neighbor's vineyard the exact moment the Prince would be riding through.

As the Prince indeed with his guards happened to ride through the vineyard; Cinderella made sure her attire insinuate her to be a "sweet country Nobel" for she knew she'd catch his eye. And when she did... The Prince slowed down to "respectfully greet a lady".

"Pardon me my Lady, but what is a Nobel doing this far out in the vineyards accompanied by no servants?" said the Prince.

Cinderella curtsied and most properly said, "Tis Lady Frella your Majesty and I beg your pardon. I was most enjoying the countryside and need a moment to myself." Cinderella then made sure she confidently and with slight seduction said, "Don't *you* ever desire to be away from your servants...alone with your thoughts your Majesty?"

"It's Alonso Madame, and I do sometimes...as if that were actually possible." said the Prince in the most proper, but flirtatious, manor. And that was the beginning of a complicated romance.

Prince Alonso looked different than her Cinderboy. He had dark brown sexy skin with dark brown hair and dark brown eyes. He was indeed tall and sexy like William but was more built than just slender. Cinderella couldn't help but notice his books were a little charming. She was intrigued at the thought of a romance not hidden. Therefore, she couldn't help herself but to be a little more enthusiastic about seducing the Prince, as part of her plan. Cinderella knew she had to show herself "different" from all the other Nobles to keep his attention. She knew she needed to prove herself "Fit for Queen" before she even began the real seductions.

Over the next few weeks Cinderella sophistically planned to "accidentally" bump into his Royal Majesty almost every time he left the Palace. She continued to bribe his guards as she carefully knew where to place each chess piece. She thought it almost too hilarious when she playfully told Prince Alonso, "Maybe it's destiny," as he thought it "odd" they kept crossing paths. As Cinderella said this graciously she also gave Prince Alonso seductive eyes (the look in your eye that says... I royally want to fuck you). The Prince was obviously not immune to Cinderella's charm. But she knew she needed a way to get him alone without looking like a harolette. She then realized she needed to host another Swaraj but not just any party...one large enough to invite The Prince!

During her plotting to rule the entire kingdom, she had done well at avoiding her stepmother. This would normally be a happy moment for Frella. However, she knew an event of this size would require Stepmother *and* Sir Frederick's cooperation. She knew that guilt would very much be of use. Cinderella (being the chess player she was) knew to start with the weaker of her two components first... Sir Frederick. She arranged for her carriage to stop by Sir Frederick Henshaw's land on her way home. She announced herself not before waltzing in his office (as he had done her).

"Sir Fredrick! My long time and trusted friend, I think you at least owe me a small favor. Don't you?" Cinderella said spitefully.

Sir Fredrick replied in a gentlemanly manor, "Frella, I have your best interest at heart. I believe you overreacted out of grief, something I understand all too well."

Cinderella was quick to interrupt, "There's no need for courtesies. Do you have means to message your cousin, The Duke, or not?"

"Yes my Lady! Tis a fine match for you Frella... You'd be Royalty!" Sir Frederick proclaimed.

Cinderella replied, "Royalty indeed."

"Invite him to my extravagant Ball then Sir... *this* happy Friday. Invite your most prestigious friends as well. Let's make this an event for Royalty. I have already consoled Stepmother and she is delighted!" Cinderella said (as crass as she could be) as she quickly dismissed herself. She then hurried to speak with her stepmother.

She had three steps to this delicate matter: apologize, make her feel guilty, and "excite" her about the Ball by showing her interest in marriage to the Duke. Cinderella thought of what to say as she drew closer to Stepmother's quarters. Then Cinderella realized "physical affection" and tears should do nicely to convince Stepmother she was "but a girl". Therefore, she threw herself onto her stepmother's lap, like a child, and cried.

"I am so truly sorry Stepmother! You were right! You were unbelievably right about me being in no emotional state, or age, to handle these...pressures. You *are* my only family now." Cinderella proclaimed. She then lifted her head, looked at the Duchess and said, "I want to take care of you... Sir Fredrick has suggested to me an extravagant Ball! He is inviting the Duke and showing society that we are well, after Father's passing, and a prestigious union. I *will* accept the Duke's proposal, may he ask. Stepmother what do you think?" Cinderella said most intently but with most "impure" intentions.

"That's a lovely idea dear. I think tis a wonderful match for you and the Duke. And Frella, of course I forgive you." Stepmother replied sweetly as *she* thought she now controlled everything.

Cinderella was all too smart. She knew not to alert her enemies of the Prince's attendance so they could conspire. She made sure to be purchasing the finest jewelry, for her fine party, in her fine gown whist Prince Alonso was passing through. She acted most innocent and surprised as he approached her.

"Am I throwing a Ball I'm not aware of my Lady," said Prince Alonso.

She then most confidentially (as if he were no deity in her eyes) responded, "Actually your Majesty... *I* am."

"You see, I need a bit of cheering up after my father's tragic passing. All the most prestigious Nobles will be in attendance, along with The Duke of Monroe. Won't you please come?" Cinderella asked as she bat her eyes. However, Prince Alonso was uncertain of an appearance on such short notice. Cinderella then leaned a little closer and discretely (and most seductive) said, "There's plenty of ways to 'avoid' your servants and the public in *my* mansion your Grace." Prince Alonso smiled and agreed.

The Ball in the Great Hall was more than lavishing. It truly was "A Party Fit for Royals". Sir Frederick spared no expense hoping for a union with Frella and the Duke. Cinderella was actually enjoying herself and a lot of wine. She did her best to keep conversations with the Duke of Monroe brief, as she avoided him by showing "her presence was demanded by many". Continuing to swig her many, many glasses of wine, she was a little nervous the Prince would not be able to come. But just as she began to look down, her servants announced "The Prince" had arrived! Cinderella quickly found her Stepmother and *casually* said, "What a lovely surprise! He was fond of Father's research." She knew Stepmother had no time to sabotage what she didn't expect and hurried to Prince Alonso.

"Hello, Prince Alonso! Good of you to come your Grace. Welcome to my lovely home. Let me show you around." Cinderella said most enthusiastically. She first introduced him to "The Duke of Monroe" (as if it were common to host Royalty). She was having a splendid time showing him the "important and honorable" Noble she was. She took pleasure in the thought she had succeeded in her conquest...until she noticed the beautiful Ann caught his eye.

CHAPTER VII

"THE CINDERBOY"

Apparently Ann's beauty was more of a threat than Cinderella realized...this much enraged her. Cinderella knew she couldn't just poison her, nor Stepmother (even though she'd like to). She knew she must devise a plan quickly to detour Ann away from his Majesty. Cinderella also realized, she must move forward with her seduction. Cinderella thought of this as she whispered into Prince Alonso's ear, "You want to evade you guards? Walk straight, quickly, then turn right. There's a secret corridor behind the hallway mirror. I'll be just but a moment."

Cinderella then hastily sneaked her way to the Prince with her secret passages. Cinderella showed no demureness as she pushed him into a dark corner. She kissed him lustfully, as she slipped her tongue in between his lips, both of them forgot about shyness. However, he did not distract her the way William did. She quickly pulled away as Prince Alonso's hand slide closer from her waist to her thighs. "You are *not* alone in your desires your Grace. I too yearn for something...more. But I am too much of a Lady to act as a complete harolette." Cinderella said almost bashfully but with a confident demeanor. "There is much Royalty that would be pleased for my hand in marriage." She said as she giggled and bat her eyes. As she then gracefully started to walk away, she turned to the Prince and whispered (most seductive), "I'm glad you came to my party Prince Alonso."

As the Prince gave her the most smug of all grins,

Cinderella knew he was hooked to her line of bait. However, she was far too eager to teach Sweet Ann a lesson about men. At first she considered sending her dashing young stable boy to, unorthodox, seduce her stepsister. "She may not be as ignorant as her halfwit little sister, but she is innocent to the world around her never-the-less." Cinderella thought to herself. Ann was genuinely kind and gracious of others as Frella *pretended* to be. "She's just as susceptible to a boy's seduction as any maiden, perhaps more," Cinderella smiled to herself. But then Cinderella realized "so is a man", and the stable boy could not be trusted not to fall in love himself. Cinderella knew, deep in her dark heart, the only one truly devoted to her...was William. She then summoned her Cinderboy, hoping he knew *nothing* of her secret liaison with the Prince.

William was quick to lovingly crawl into bed with Cinderella and put his arms around her. He knew not of the details, but knew of her agenda and approaches with the Prince. Obviously, he was a little jealous and wanted to show Frella...*he* truly loved her. Of course our Cinderella was quite aware of this. She knew every action and thought of her William's heart. Therefore, she turned to him and began to run her fingers through his long, unstyled, blond hair.

"William my darling, YOU are my one true love. I would do anything, and everything, to be with you. I would wait a million years. I wonder though, would you go through these lengths for me?" Cinderella said passionately.

"Of course my love! How could you even ask?!" William said crossly.

Cinderella then shout, "I am FORCED to seduce another because of Stepmother! I *must* lure him. I must bed him. I must do this, so in time, as a Duke, you may marry me!" As tears began to run down her face, she then intensely said, "Now *you* must seduce and bed Ann."

"I will not!" William shout (and oh the look he gave her).

"William, she is a threat to my success with the Prince. She is a whiley temptress, like her mother, I cannot have her ruin our only chance!" Cinderella said persistently. She then kissed the left side of his neck...then the right, softly. And then Cinderella whispered gently into her Cinderboy's ear, "It's just once my darling, just once. Please. I love you...until the end of all time. But you MUST warm her heart, then her bed." William nodded in agreement as Cinderella kissed him lustfully. She then said, "Think of us now even on the chess board my darling... Ann for the Prince."

The next morning Cinderella made sure the Senior housemaid sent the Cinderboy to sweep Ann's room (so he did not forget his purpose). Over the next few days, with Cinderella pressuring him, it did not take Ann long to start giving him a few lustful glances. William complimented her day by day, letting her "regardless of status" he was not frightened to notice her beauty. A brave man is seductive to a women. Cinderella knew this as she knew his charms would work on Sweet Ann (as they did her). As William pushed Cinderella up against the wall of the cooking quarters (as usual), Cinderella told William he must move forward with his seductions.

"A few coy glances and lustful gazes is not enough my darling," said Cinderella as she passionately kissed William.

This obviously upset him. So she grabbed his dirty

cinder hand and rubbed it, slow, up her thigh (letting William know she care not of her fine gown today). "You must touch my darling. *Your* touch...is everything." She gasped as she slightly moaned while he kissed her neck. Then she continued to seductively speak, "You must accidentally bump her, just so, spilling your cinders on her. Then as you're rapidly trying to dust them off...look into her eyes and pretend it's me. Then you softly brush the cinders off her, with your soft, long sexy hands. I want you to stare into her eyes, as if you love her, and say, 'Pardon me Madame.'" She then shed a glistening tear, starred deep in his eyes and said, "And William...promise to remember that you are mine." She then pulled him into their secret passage to make love to him (and remind him who he loved).

William followed Frella's instructions the next day. Sweet Ann no doubtable gazed back at William and stopped his touch not. Cinderella knew this would have happened. Therefore, that night informed William, "Now for the kiss my darling. All it will take is one kiss my darling and her heart will drop as mine did. When she looks at you again tomorrow with affection in her eyes...you grab her and you push your body against hers. You kiss her, plunging your sweet tongue in between her lips so she may taste your flavor! You kiss he neck...like mine. You will then rub your hands up her soft thighs and up to her flower...then pluck it! If you have any trouble in this...just think of how I must seduce Prince Alonso. Oh and Darling...bring me her sash when you succeed."

William, so confused with love for Frella and anger towards her stepfamily (for her having to seduce the Prince) did as he was told. The graceful yet curious and enticed Ann did not refuse him. How could she? After all

Cinderboy "obviously" had his charms. He grabbed Ann he, looked at her and starred. Then he kissed her forcefully, as he indeed, plunged his tongue between her lips. Ann so unworldly had never felt like this before and was most enticed by William. She kissed him back enjoying his tongue. William then proceeded to kiss her neck and seduce her. His soft lips were warm upon her neck as he imagined she were Frella. Her breathing became more heavy and rapid, as did her heart. William just wanted to be done with Ann so he could hurry back to matters at hand. Therefore he quickly rubbed his long, slender fingers up Ann's garters and in between her legs. He wasted no time entering her as he threw her unto the wall. Ann moaned louder and her body shook as he recklessly thrusted. As he pulled Ann to a halt and kissed her with passion, he wished it were Frella. He wasted no time retrieving her sash as he dashed back to Cinderella.

When William returned to Cinderella with Ann's sash as promised she held him. She loved him and comforted him as she watched his innocence die a little (as hers had long ago). This saddened Cinderella as she kissed him and said, "You are my one *true* love." However, she couldn't help but be a little happy inside…for her plan to hurt Sweet Ann run so much deeper. She wanted to enjoy breaking Ann's "pure heart", as she remove it from the chess board to get closer to the King. Cinderella was the kind of girl who let nothing get in her way. Did you think she became Queen by being sweet and having a fairy Godmother? Please.

But as always, she never led her William to believe she enjoyed being cruel.

CHAPTER VIII

"ANN'S PURE HEART"

William usually awoke a few hours earlier than Frella to sneak out of their secret passage and begin his chores. He would always let Cinderella sleep as his kiss her forehead when he left. However... Since he was so upset the night before, Cinderella knew she must awaken to inform him of his next task (since he had had time to rest and gather himself). Therefore, this particular morning William awoke to Cinderella kissing his forehead.

"I am happy to wake to *your* face my love," said William.

"I love you more than anyone my darling, and I am truly sorry about yesterday. It has ached my heart all night. William, will you please make yourself scarce to everyone but me the next few days?" Cinderella said sorrowfully.

William gazed into her mournful eyes, with his gorgeous dark green eyes. He then softly agreed, "Of course my love." He then gently touched Cinderella's face, pushed her hair back and kissed her deeply.

Cinderella was pleased watching Ann the next few days. She could practically see Ann glowing with a newfound happiness. She deceitfully smirked at the thought of taking it away. She then laughed at the thought of Sweet Ann wondering where her newfound love was. Cinderella had of course enjoyed laying with her Cinderboy almost all day and night for the past two days. But, she knew "it was time" to continue her plot (for she had intentionally wanted him to "desert" Sweet Ann all along).

"William my darling, I wish it could be like this every day." Cinderella said lovingly.

"So do I," William replied sincerely.

"If that is true, then you must go to Ann...tonight! You must break her heart that you have warmed. You must scold her for being the whore that she is. Everything you tell her WILL be true. You must condemn her for her wicked ways, so that she will grieve. This will knock her off the chess board long enough for me to become Queen. Only then will I have the power to save our home...to entitle you to a status that NO ONE could deny our marriage my darling." Cinderella said most imperative as she bat her eyes. William looked at Cinderella gravely and said, "What would you have me do my love."

"You will go surprise her when everyone sleeps. She *will* be happy to see you. But, you will tell her you're disgusted with yourself for sleeping with a whore who would give herself to you so freely. You will tell her, regardless of status, you could never love a whore who probably lays with every handsome servant she sees. And as sure as she is a liar, she will deny this. You then tell her along with being a spoiled snob (and a whore), that she is the stupidest girl you have ever met. I mean, to sleep with you so quickly after you compliment her pretty face, which is sadly all she will ever be. You then leave the room rapidly. Do you understand my darling?" Cinderella said determinedly.

William nodded in agreement and, of course, Cinderella insisted that he practice these words before heading to Ann's quarters. This brought Cinderella much pleasure...to destroy Ann's pure heart. And she conspired to have even more pleasure embarrassing Ann the next day and bending her to her will (with a little extortion). After all, knowledge is power. And Cinderella LOVED a good scandal while eliminating the competition. So she took a secret passage leading right above Ann's room so she could witness and enjoy William's torture.

Cinderella contained her giggles with most difficulty as she was eaves dropping. She overheard Sweet Ann crying and proclaiming her virginity. Cinderella then had the largest smile as Ann said, "I thought I was special. I thought you loved me." In which William replied, "That's what a wench like you gets for thinking. Perhaps you should continue to practice what your more suited for...spreading your legs." Cinderella dashed back up to her quarters so she could laugh hysterically and enjoy this moment. She then lie in bed starring at Ann's dirty sash as she could not wait 'til morning.

Cinderella was dressed in her finest before the sun rose. She told William to ensure no servants came to dress Ann that morning until they were summoned by *her*. And as Ann awoke that morning, after crying herself to sleep, she was horrified to see Frella standing in front of her twirling her sash (like a windmill)...with cinders on it.

"Well, well, well," said Cinderella taunting Ann. The mortified and frightened Ann knew not what to do besides burst into tears. Poor Ann, so gentle in nature, had too learned a lesson about a man's scorn...that Cinderella was all too happy to teach her. She was hurt, humiliated and most of all frightened of Cinderella. Cinderella, the wicked and jealous girl she was, slithered close to Ann's face like a snake. She grabbed Ann's pretty little chin as she was close enough to kiss her and whispered, "Crying won't save you. Listen to me and listen well, I saw the Prince eye your pretty face. He would NEVER marry a Cinderboy's whore. You act graceful. Yet, YOU are truly filth in the dirt. Now," Cinderella smiled sweetly and changed tone, "you will tell the Prince you grieve for your dead betrothed and are far too depressed to leave your quarters may he come around. You will FORGET my Cinderboy and NEVER look his way again. That is...if you *still* want to be considered a Lady. Do you understand?" Cinderella said vindictively. The scared and distraught Ann nodded in agreement. Cinderella was happy to leave her quarters and summon Ann's dress maids as she had much "Royal Seduction" to arrange.

Little did Cinderella know...a glance was but a glance. And she had forever tainted her and her Cinderboy's once pure love for not. For the Prince, after Cinderella's Ball...was intrigued by *her*.

heavy, hot...and deep. But her seductive stare quickly turned into an innocent one. She then spoke, "You think of me a harolette now?" Prince Alonso responded, "Frella, I think of you as anything but." Cinderella smiled sweetly but with much deceit, as she knew she was all the more closer to becoming Queen. Prince Alonso smiled back and (of course) said, "I want to be inside you my Lady." Cinderella couldn't help but chuckle. The Prince was just so proper compared to her Cinderboy. She then realized she was going to much enjoy being the more "dominant" one...for once. She then thought it most hilarious to say, "You can fuck me when you love me." She made sure to then bat her eyes as she paused and said, "Your Grace." Cinderella of course enjoyed this torture.

"I'm not sure I understand what love is Frella. We are not as 'passionate' in the Palace as you. I've never met a Lady as bold as the Frella. I might not be certain of what love is...but I think I love you," said Prince Alonso most sincere. Cinderella bursting with the joy of success contained herself not. She smiled grandly with true happiness! And, as she could not help herself, ran her tongue up his neck then took his mouth and kissed him so lustful it was obscene! Just then Cinderella caught herself and remembered William (and her goals). She then replied, "If you love me, Alonso, you'd call me your Queen before entering me. I cannot completely give myself to you...yet. I am the richest Nobel Heir of this land your Grace (as she bat her eyes), not a halfwit Palace maid." Cinderella grinned jolly as she said this *knowing* she was enchanting and adorable.

Prince Alonso smiled sweetly. He could not resist Frella's "outspoken" persona and charm. He gently rubbed his fingers on her face and kissed her. He opened his mouth to speak but Cinderella immediately interrupted.

"Your Majesty I must go!" she said frantically. She then changed to a serious tone and said, "You have your duties and I have mine."

Prince Alonso nodded in agreement as he lifted Cinderella unto his steed. His Majesty then mounted himself unto the horse as put Frella's arms around his waist while they whipped away. Cinderella had of course interrupted him on purpose. For she knew he needed time to think of her "proposal"...before he made his. She was ever so pleased with herself. For Cinderella also knew... when Prince Alonso put her hand around his waist, as if he were claiming her, that he was indeed in love. As I said, she *was* more than pleased with herself but was eager to return home to her true love William.

When Prince Alonso returned her to her carriage in the town square, he asked Frella when he would see her again. Cinderella knew that he would, of course, and was more than happy to respond, "When you decide what you truly desire your grace." She giggled and blew him a kiss as her carriage began to ride off. Cinderella could not hardly wait to go home to her Cinderboy whom she loved. It was almost as if she felt a little guilt for her "royal seduction"...*almost*. The Prince with his *dark beauty* had indeed turned Cinderella on. But, so wrapped up in William she was yearning for *him* to finish her off! For evil as she may be...she loved her Cinderboy.

Over the next few days Cinderella gave Prince Alonso time to suffer. She knew very well, after her teasing he would come to her as any man. And sure enough he sent her a Royal Message to meet her in the neighboring vineyard. Stepmother, with intentions of her own, inquired about the messenger at the door. Cinderella with her charming wits replied, "Tis from the Duke! He wishes to meet with me...probably to propose! Wish me luck Stepmother for this family WILL live well" as she scurried out the door to leave on her horse. Her wicked Stepmother was all too happy thinking "She" had arranged this match.

Cinderella, eager for vengeance, waist no more time in her "Royal Seduction". The moment she seen Prince Alonso waiting by the apple tree (where they first met), she rushed to him dominantly grabbing him towards her loins! She kissed him heavy and deep then bit his neck. She wasted no time lifting her leg up high, around his waist. Her hand rubbed quickly down his muscles and chest to his cock! She forcefully pushed him inside her as she pulled him against the apple tree. She bit the back of his neck harder as he knew she wanted him to thrust deeper!

She then seductively whispered in his ear, "Tell me when you're going to finish my Prince" as Prince Alonso pounded in and out of her more and more rapid. And more engorged was he than her Cinderboy... It was then Cinderella fell a little into seduction herself. Prince Alonso then began to moan, "There it goes. There it goes!" Cinderella then quickly moaned, "Tell me you love me." As he spilled inside her he gasped and spoke, "I love you!" Cinderella grabbed his face with both hands and stuck her tongue in his mouth as she kissed him hard.

Prince Alonso was enchanted! He gentle touch Frella's face and said, "I wish you to be *mine* forever... Marry me Lady Frella."

CHAPTER X

"ROYAL INTRODUCTIONS"

Cinderella ecstatic with the joy of conquest was more than eager to return home and inform her wicked Stepmother of her defeat. And, of course…plan her Royal Wedding.

"Stepmother! I have the most wonderful news!" Cinderella spoke ever so sweetly. But only she was aware of her sarcasm. Her wicked stepmother most delightfully responded, "You have accepted the Duke's proposal?" She tried to hide her wicked agenda and not sound too eager to get her hands on the Duke's coins. Cinderella was almost too thirsty (craving the taste of victory). She acted so innocent…so sincere, and said, "Oh Stepmother, we will ALL be Royalty and live well…for I am to be your Queen!"

Stepmother was astonished. She did not like the thought of this "stupid country Nobel" ruling the Kingdom…ruling *her*, not to mention she was extremely confused.

"What?" She responded trying to keep her couth.

"Well, I suppose the Prince was enticed after my Ball. He stopped my carriage on the way to the Duke of Monroe." Cinderella stated while batting her eyes (as if she were truly surprised of this).

Stepmother was happy they would obviously be living well, yet had a curious doubt in the back of her mind. Cinderella, much so desirous to put her enemies in their place, was quick to inform Stepmother that the Royal Carriage would arrive in the morning to take her along with chosen servants to the Palace. She made it quite clear she would "waste not time" becoming Queen. She then rushed upstairs to "collect her things" but in reality she had to rush to William.

Her Cinderboy, however, was already waiting in their secret quarters. He had been wondering, with much distress, of her "Royal affairs". Cinderella knew immediately by the look on his face...she must remind him of "their" love and "their" goals.

"William my darling, we have succeeded! I love you so much. I am Queen now my love. Soon enough, you will be a grand Duke and we can be happy together!" Cinderella brushed his gorgeous, long, unstyled blond hair back kissing his neck as she said this. She seductively whispered into his ear, "Your Queen will need a Royal Taylor to reach up my royal dresses my darling." William, of course giving in to her, kissed her with a love that was more than love.

The next morning when the carriage arrived, Cinderella was more than eager to enter with her Cinderboy and two stable boys of course. For the new Queen need her "own" Royal Guards to be her eyes and ears of the Palace. As she enjoyed the ride she already had a million ideas for her "Royal Wedding"...along with her Royal Revenge! She knew she must gather herself, however, before meeting the King. After all, seducing the young Prince is one thing. But, proving herself "fit to rule" the ENTIRE Kingdom to the King might *actually* take a little effort. For Cinderella was a smart enough chess player to realize this.

As she enter the Palace dressed in the most elegant of modern and sexy gowns, she knew she must act "as Queen". Why would the King desire a "simple" girl to rule? She could not show her fear. Everyone knew the Queen had been gone for quite some time (something her and Prince Alonso had in common). Cinderella thought it rather obvious the Kingdom needed a "motherly" hand.

The King, however, had many things on his mind as well...and not about his son's marriage. When Prince Alonso escorted Frella to meet his father, he introduced King Antonio of Spain to her. Cinderella nervously curtsied and spoke, "Tis my honor to meet the man that raised Alonso. I love him dear sir as I have loved this land. And, I am most ambitious to prove my dedication."

The King was indeed impressed by her tact and couldn't help but to reply, "My so outspoken my Lady!" He looked at Prince Alonso and said, "Like your mother... I see the attraction." Prince Alonso smiled thinking his dad was sincere. The King then changed to a more sarcastic and belittling tone and said, "Now my dear... my son, so spoiled and knowing nothing of how to rule, is too busy gallivanting to notice we have bad blood with the Northerners. They are not our 'official' enemies but this Kingdom needs another war not! Can *you* prove your dedication and tell me what to do? My Royal Advisors are idiots at best."

Thank goodness our dark Cinderella was indeed no dumb country girl and more that "creative" under pressure.

She, with most respect and grace, instantly replied, "That's simple your Majesty. Invite them to the grandest wedding this Kingdom has *ever* seen...to discuss peace and friendship of course." Knowing she had succeeded in impressing the King Cinderella smiled ever so sweet.

King Antonio was speechless! He paused, then looked at Frella with sincere happiness (for he had, in a sense, "fallen in love" with our temptress as well). He laughed and told his son, "Looks like our new Queen will be advising *you*! Son she is most intelligent and un-questionably fit to rule." He then looked back at Frella and said, "My dear I think you just prevented a war. I most certainly want Norway to meet you! Tell our Pal-ace staff ANY ideas you have for this *Grand* wedding."

Cinderella now knowing (even the King!) would lis-ten to *her*, having so much sin in her grin, happily re-plied, "Oh, I certainly have plans your Majesty."

CHAPTER XI

"THE ROYAL WEDDING PART 1"

The day of the Royal Wedding was by all means... "Perfect". Cinderella's wedding gown had been sent to het by France. Tis was the latest of all fashions, of course. It showed a bit more of her cleavage and body than a traditional wedding gown. But...this was a Grand Wedding to be remembered, and Cinderella wanted to show the Kingdom had style. It was gorgeous! The bottom, so stylish, not too many ruffles but just so. Yet it was extravagantly wide...her Cinderboy (now Royal Taylor) could fit underneath it. As he feel the core of her moisture til it was dripping wet the other maids know not! William could not help but to have a taste while he was down there, for Cinderella smelled of the rose bath she'd been given for this day. But, as he moved his tongue more rapidly in swirling motions until Cinderella could take no more, she contained her moans not. She immediately sent the other servants oust.

"William!" She shrieked and giggled. He arose and kissed her with passion. Cinderella loved him so. But, as she kissed his soft lips she stopped. She looked into his deep green eyes and said, "You know I'd rather be with you tonight my darling."

William looked down as he was reminded *he* was not the one she was marrying and said, "I know."

"William...today is imperative! After today I will waste no time with Royal Proclamations lover. Ok?" Cinderella spoke softly. She did not ever want her Cinderboy upset. "Look at this dress!" She tried to jest. "I can't wait for those to wicked little whores to carry it behind me," she laughed with William and kissed him again. It was a great honor to be in the Royal Ceremony holding the Queen's dress train. However, Cinderella spitefully gave her stepsister's this honor...knowing their place was behind her. Cinderella then dismissed William for she had a lot to do on this day.

As she walk down the aisle, the Palace was decorated to perfection. Frella insisted on white oleanders everywhere. There must have been a million white candles aligned perfectly on each side along with at least a dozen chandeliers all filled with small white candles as well. The Royal Scientist had some special entertainment planned to consummate the marriage and announce the Royal Reception. They were called "Royal Fireworks" and were acquired from China.

Prince Alonso was so in love with Cinderella. To the common eye not knowing what lies beneath, the ceremony was of two young lovers and most romantic.

As they share the drink of their wine cup and promised their mutual love both in prosperity and adversity... The Priest pronounced the couple man and wife and invoked God's blessing upon them. Just then, behind them, in both corners of the Great Hall the Royal Fireworks were lit. It was an amazing stream of lights, smoke and noise as Alonso and Frella kissed. There were floating colors of orange, red, green and purple. The crowd was more than impressed, they were amazed.

Cinderella knew how to throw a party and impress the Northerners. King Antonio made certain Frella sat next to Northern Royalty placing her directly next to King Albert of Norway. Acting ignorant of "bad blood" Cinderella seductively but most cunningly charmed him. "I'm so pleased you came to my wedding your Majesty. I am more than honored Queen to make some new friends. This Kingdom needed a woman's touch." Cinderella made sure to gracefully hold his hand as she said this...and by graceful I mean slyly seductive.

"Now that I am Queen I want to bring this Kingdom into modern society. Starting by making new *allies* and peace." She bat her eyes and said this. Therefore, King Albert was indeed enticed by Frella's beauty and boldness (just like everyone else). Cinderella then thought it clever to say, "We so need trustworthy friends your Majesty. It has been said, by a few, that we might have enemies. But I can see *you* are not. You are much too charming and advanced your Majesty. It is very clear you are as much as a 'visionary' as I." The King of Norway giggled in flattery as they tip their wine cups in cheers.

Cinderella then thought it prudent to ask, "So tell me of *your* wedding customs your Majesty." Little did Cinderella know it was a "good luck" custom in the North to break a cake over the brides head. Cinderella knew she must not stop "impressing" the enemies, not for two seconds. Being the Lady she was, Frella did not want the cake to ruin her perfect hair nor perfect gown; for she had not had enough wine to *not* detest this. However, she was a girl with goals. She then made the announcement to ALL, "They were honoring their new friends by performing a Northern good luck tradition."

With everything on her mind, she was in no mood to look like a "kitchen maid" at her elaborate Royal Wedding. Prince Alonso, thinking Frella was a sweet and adventurous girl laughed in joy. He was truly having fun with his "jolly" new bride. Cinderella laughed and smiled so fair but so falsely. As she dismissed herself to "freshen up", she thought no one could possibly hear her undertones over all the excitement. She walked off thinking out loud to herself that the Northerners were barbarians and their King a fat pervert.

As she returned, after many dress maids quickly sponged her and dressed her in a dazzling Ball gown, she was pleased. For Cinderella had indeed thrown a "Grand Wedding". There was a magnificent feast, jousting, fine banqueting and foreign entertainment. She sat back down, next to King Albert of course, to enjoy another cup of wine. Yes, everything was "perfect" until...

CHAPTER XII

"THE ROYAL WEDDING PART 2"

"You will hold your tongue Sir or I shall cut it out!" Cinderella heard the voice of Drake (her favored Stable Boy and now Royal Guard) shouting.

"And I'll cut out your fucking heart! You people have always thought you are better than us! Our King might be jolly and fat...but your Queen shows enough body to put our whores to shame!" A Northerner shouted this at her Stable Boy.

Cinderella then heard the screams of her people and *both* sides draw their weapons! For Drake had daggered the Northerner and pushed his lifeless body, off the blade, onto the ground. King Albert immediately stood up as did Queen Frella. He raised his hand in signal for his men to halt as did King Antonio. Cinderella, not thinking twice before acting, immediately shout, "Everyone...STAND DOWN! This is a celebration and time of peace!" Just then several Northerners shout, "No peace! There can be no peace!" King Albert informed them to let Queen Frella speak.

"I know we have bad blood and many different customs. But *I* am Queen now. And I happen to think You Northerners are fun, daring and honorable young men! I invited you here to share this Kingdom's joy with you. I desire more than anything that you PLEASE accept my friendship. For with your bravery and Spain's advances... We are *both* more powerful together as a GRAND UNION!" Cinderella spoke as a natural born leader. Everyone was charmed by Frella's kind words. (She then knew it wise shed a few tears) as she then, so gently, held King Albert's hand in both of hers and said directly to him...

"My guard will be imprisoned and stand a *very* just and fair trial I assure you. Your Majesty... I am so sorry."

Although King Albert was clearly outraged by the clash he allowed Cinderella's charm to soothe him. After all the Northerner dead was not Royalty, therefore, there was no "immediate' war. Cinderella knew she must throw in a slight bit of seduction to "assure" peace. So she slowly and shyly provocative leaned her breasts towards King Albert as she kissed bye on his cheek with her soft sexy lips. King Albert then dismissed his men and himself as the other Royal Guards escorted Drake to the jail underneath the Palace. Now that the drama was finally over Prince Alonso rushed to Frella's table to comfort his new bride, after a "not so perfect" wedding.

King Antonio (probably on the verge of a heart attack) was immediately escorted back to his Royal Chambers. Prince Alonso rubbed Cinderella's face, ever so gently, and said, "Frella you were brilliant! I am more than proud to call you my Queen! Are you alright my Queen?" Just then as she was about to kiss her new husband she saw William standing in the distance and quickly run off to quarters. She then realized that even with the Kingdom on the brink of war...*his* chambers was where she really wanted to be on her wedding night. She then looked down at the ground, in distress, and realized... she had the "perfect excuse" to do what she wanted to.

Cinderella then looked up at Prince Alonso shedding many "fake" tears and said, "Oh darling! I'm so upset! I put on a brave face, like a good Queen, but I was so scared for all our lives!" Then she hugged him and cried (like a damsel in distress). "Our wedding has been utterly ruined!" Cinderella shout. She then told him she needed to be alone tonight to think...for he knew the inside of her body anyway. Prince Alonso, so sincerely enchanted by Frella, did as she requested and dismissed himself to his Royal Quarters. Our evil Cinderella dismissed herself to hers as well...while she sneakily had her other Stable Boy escort her to her "Royal Taylor's" chambers. Drake's younger brother, Alejandro (now Royal Guard #2), of course stood guard outside. She needed much protection of her and William, eyes and ears, for they were no longer in her mansion.

She was, in that moment, truly happy to see her Cinderboy (and true love) sleeping as she enter his chambers. She quickly slithered her body in bed, next to his. She rubbed his long, unstyled, blond hair behind his ears and whispered seductively...softly, and slowly, "I love you forever and always." William's large sexy eyes were widened as he awoke to Cinderella.

"Frella are you mad?! What are you doing here on your wedding night my love?!" William whispered intently. He was obviously filled with joy, however, he was more concerned with his true love's safety. Cinderella immediately put her hands over his mouth to silence him.

She wasted no more time kissing him. She gently slipped her tongue in his mouth as she grabbed his face with both hands. She leaned in to kiss him harder and hotter as she straddled him. She starred in his gorgeous, green eyes and said, "I told you this morning... I'd rather be with *you*. Now finish what you started earlier today my darling."

She was feeling a little more "bossy" after her first night as Queen. She then gently sucked his top lip...then the bottom before placing her tongue in between them. William loved her tongue as he loved her deeply. He pulled her body closer to him with both hands and threw her onto the other side of the bed to dominate her. He bit the back of her neck as he grinded slowly on top of her. Cinderella almost soaked her undergarments in wetness for she *loved* when her Cinderboy bit her neck. He then slowly kissed back from her lower neck to her mouth as he pinched her nipples gently. His big lips were so, so soft as he quickly kissed down from to her nipples then down in between her thighs. His tongue flickered up and down more rapidly then he slid it inside her. He then licked his tongue back up and in circular motions as he pressed his tongue and mouth harder against her. Cinderella spilled in his mouth with her moister. William enjoyed her taste and arose to kiss her lustfully (as he expected no favors in return for he only cared for Cinderella's happiness). William slipped immediately his cock inside her and thrusted slowly as he kissed her with force and passion. He grinded inside her softly as he "perfectly" curved his pelvic to make love to her. Cinderella knew her Cinderboy loved her fingernails in his back so she clawed both his shoulders and pulled down. His curving strokes hit her inside spot perfectly, and felt so good, that she contained her moans not. But as she scratched his back his thrusts became faster and harder. William's breathing became more rapid and heavy as he began to grunt. He then reached his fingers down to rub the top of her as he more forcefully pounded in and out of her. He started to rub faster back and forth as he flickered his fingers. Cinderella gasped and shrieked when she orgasmed rapidly flowing out like a waterfall. Her Cinderboy could always feel on his engorged cock when she finished. He then pressed his long slender fingers down harder and continued to rub fast as he thrusted deeper! He kissed Cinderella heavy and deep as he spilled inside her pulling her hips close!

— *C.H.Darkling* —

CHAPTER XIII

"A WICKED REIGN"

Cinderella had left William's quarters quickly last night and spoke not of her "tragically ruined wedding". For he had given her all the comfort she *truly* needed. And this morning she was "truly" ready to begin her wicked reign and set her status as Queen!

For now that Cinderella has satisfied her body (and her need to lie with her Cinderboy her wedding night), Cinderella indeed needed to satisfy her thirst for vengeance! As I said before, our dark Cinderella was vengeful and sinister. She was so truly evil that she knew... She could not even think about foreign enemies before "removing her near-at-hand enemies first". And who was it that deserved her wrath before Stepmother? Sir Fredrick Henshaw of course!

"My betrayers shall pay first now that I'm Queen! He dare conspire with that whore...to steal from me?! And sell me off, like a cow, to that little troll of a Duke! Oh, Sir Fredrick... YOU are about to lose everything!" Cinderella humbled to herself. But then she began to think, "I must dispose of him publically for Stepmother to see..." Then her face brightened and almost glowed as she said to herself, "I think a public hanging will do nicely."

Cinderella then realized she needed to call forth for a trial. Just then, she remembered her favored Stable Boy, Drake. "This all started because *my* servant honored me." She thought to herself. She then thought of the perfect pitch to tell the King for a "trial". So she raced to have an audience with her new father-in-law.

"King Antonio!" Cinderella said gracefully as she enter the Royal Headquarters of the Palace. "I already know how to put this Kingdom at ease your Majesty, I have been thinking all night." She stated regally.

King Antonio ordered his advisors (that were screaming "war") to silence, as he took Cinderella under his arm (wishing his own child had half her brains and boldness). "Yes my dear, we are happy to hear our new Queen's opinion," he shout. He then under toned whispered how proud he was of her last night.

"Well, we must show this Kingdom, we are a strong and just Dynasty THAT WILL protect our people from harm!" Cinderella shout most imperative.

"Now Frella, I'm sure you have an answer... How can we achieve this without war your Highness?" King Antonio graciously spoke to her as a father figure.

"A Fair Trial your Majesty." Cinderella smirked as she said this. For she knew, she was about to set her mark and the "Royal Idiots/Advisors" in their place.

"A trail for what?" One Advisor shouted. "Our young Queen is worried of playing politics but NOT the matter at hand," another shouted. Cinderella glared at him with rage then politely smiled. King Antonio raised his hand, to silence, and said, "Go on."

Cinderella walked up right behind her martyrs and shout firmly to her peers, "How can we protect *our* people from war if we are not at peace with ourselves? Hmmm? Let's have a Public Trial showing that MY reign does not tolerate rapists, treason...or molesters! Let us show the people this Kingdom is based on loyalty, pride and honor!" The room became silent. Cinderella then walked closer to father-in-law and said, "As far as my Royal

Guard, whom I grew up with, goes your Majesty... Let's give the Kingdom a good laugh at the barbaric Northerners. Let us show OUR people do NOT get punished for defending the honor of this Dynasty." She smiled as she said this. He indeed smiled back and bowed to *her*. All the Royal Advisors had no choice, of course, but to bow as their King did (in gratitude to Queen Frella).

Cinderella could in no way pass up an opportunity to be a "Royal Bitch" to the Royal Advisors. "Thank you your Majesty," she said so polite. She then, so *sickly sweet*, said, "I hope the supposedly smartest men in the Kingdom do not make the mistake of underestimating your 'young Queen' again." She smiled very pretty as she then softly said, "You're all dismissed... NOW," she changed to a demanding tone.

King Antonio snickered as she reminded him of his late and "outspoken" wife. He was also very impressed with his new "daughter" taking her place as Queen and "commanding the dogs".

"Your Majesty, I have a personal matter to discuss." Frella said intently. "I have long heard rumors of a degenerate that neighbored my father's land. My servants told me he...forces young servant boys to satisfy his sick and unspeakable sex games," said Cinderella. She then gravely held King Antonio's hand and bat her eyes as she said, "Your Majesty...those poor children. We must stop him and show our people we care." This much distressed the King and he agreed with Frella for a "Public Trial" in front of Spain's Dynasty in the morning.

The Royal court was all in attendance at the trail the next morning. Sir Fredrick had been arrested by the Royal Guards at dawn. And Stepmother, of course, received her invitation by Cinderella's Royal Guard last night.

"Sir Fredrick Henshaw... Come forth!" Cinderella was more than happy to shout. He walked forward and bowed in her presence. He kept his head down for he knew his fate.

"Good Sir, you have been accused of sexually abusing young servants. You are accused of harming young men in the most sick and unspeakable way. How do you plea?" stated King Antonio. King Antonio sat on his throne directly in front of the accused. Prince Alonso stood on his right and Queen Frella stood to his left. Sir Fredrick most properly and with couth replied, "I am the richest Nobel in the land. I can have any woman I desire and am NOT guilty of such crimes. I am a good man!"

Cinderella, so evil in nature, leaned towards King Antonio and whispered, "Forgive me your Majesty...for my pride. I was embarrassed. But, he made inappropriate gestures towards me when I was a very young girl and Father was away. He IS guilty. Let Your new Queen punish him...please." The King nodded in agreement.

"Sir Fredrick..." Cinderella snarled. "Men like you sicken me," she then shout and make eye contact with the Royal Court. "Our Kingdom is based on honor and justice, NOT sex slaves, abuse or greed! As your new Queen I will give Punishment Due to such criminals. The people rich...or born of servitude deserve protection!" Cinderella shout louder and louder. The court cheered in agreeance charmed by Cinderella. "Sir Fredrick Henshaw...you ARE guilty! I hereby strip you of all your titles and estates and I grant them to your honorable neighbor 'The Duchess of Frey'. And, to ensure our poor children are safe...a public hanging!" She stated enthusiastically. Sir Fredrick Henshaw became frantic as he shout and resisted the Royal Guards carrying him away.

"Drake Penya… Come Forth," Cinderella state calmly now that one of her enemies were out of the way. "You are accused of murder of one of the Norway guests at my wedding. What were you doing? Why would you dagger him Sir?" Cinderella bat her eyes as she was obviously being sarcastic in tone.

"Protecting my Queen's honor your Highness," said Drake in all seriousness as he kneeled in respect.

Cinderella smiled wickedly as she lovely replied, "Well then…you are free to go. And, you are of course reinstated in my Royal Guard. Your time has been served…and thank you. We do not punish loyalty to our good name here Sir!" She then began to laugh and say, "We can now tell our *friends* we indeed had a *Fair Trial.*" The entire Royal Courtship laughed and was jolly, except Cinderella's wicked Stepmother in the distance. She was smart enough to know Sir Fredrick's estate was not ALL she was going to receive from her new evil stepdaughter and Queen.

CHAPTER **XIV**

"BATTLE ROYALE"

Stepmother tumbled blindly, and fast, into fear and obsession. Stepmother is now quite aware of how dangerous Frella could really be quickly took over Sir Fredrick's mansion. She spent most of her time there, away from the property she had taken from our dark Cinderella. She felt safe enough away from *Frella's* servants. Over the next few weeks she plotted, indulged in her fear, how she could ensure her life. She left Ann, of course, in charge of Cinderella's mansion.

As Cinderella gave her wicked stepmother time to suffer and coil; she much enjoyed her new status as Queen. She had already sent news of a "Fair Trial" to King Albert along with gifts (offerings of peace) to keep the North at bay. And although she more than loved her Cinderboy, she was having fun enjoying Prince Alonso's larger endowment. She enjoyed his public love for her (something she couldn't have with William). However, she dare not lead William to believe she enjoyed Prince Alonso in any way.

Since the Palace was far more inconspicuous than their mansion, it was easy to convince William how they could not be together every night (without upsetting him). Cinderella hated to see her Cinderboy upset. And she cherished every moment she could sneak off with her beloved Cinderboy.

Yes, our lusty Queen was rather enjoying herself as her wicked stepmother plot. The Duchess was indeed at a standstill until one day she realized... If depriving Cinderella's servants of comfort, safety or even their lives meant saving hers...so be it!

It was in that moment she insisted her daughters be more comfortable at Sir Frederick's unoccupied mansion. Therefore, she could be as cruel as necessary to discover any incriminating information on Cinderella. She started with the Hierarchy Kitchen Maid. She knew Cinderella spent far too much time down in the cooking quarters for a Nobel girl. The maid Margaretta was an easy target, for she was a very heavy and older lady. Stepmother ensured she starve for a few days. One of the younger maids, Mary, whom was treated well by Cinderella, informed the Duchess that Queen Frella would not stand for this! The wicked Stepmother whipped the girl until she bleed all over her entire body then dismissed her and her servitude.

Mary wanted to send a message to Queen Frella, but knew it had to be unread by anyone else, and that would be difficult. Cinderella was wise enough to send one of the Stable Boy's to check on the mansion (not trusting Stepmother). However, those visits were only once every few weeks. By that time it would, of course, be too late for poor Margaretta.

After a few days too many, the poor elderly and out of shape kitchen maid was choking on her own vomit. Her body could not handle her containment and starvation. On the brink of death the maid could not bare anymore. She pleaded for her life and she yelled at the Duchess. She finally screamed at the top of her lungs, "She lays with her Cinderboy at night!"

"Lies!" Stepmother shrieked in anger. For she thought the "old bag of lard" was lying to save her own skin. She could not believe something "too good to be true".

"Tis the truth! She is in love with him. Ask any servant whom we call CINDERELLA. Ask them! Please! Please! Let me go!" Margaretta screamed in agony.

The Duchess released the bolts on the privacy room's door and immediately made arrangements to "visit the Palace". She deranged by fear of what her evil stepdaughter Queen would do...she could not bring herself to be happy of this news, for she feared it to be untrue. Then she began to think, "So what if they are rumors none-the-less. These allegations are all I need to cause complications for this evil little girl regardless!" She then uttered to herself, "I will stand my ground and threaten to implement our Queen's new reign!" She was happy as she thought of this and smirked. Stepmother, of course, relished the thought of being in control of everything once more.

That very evening she was dressed in the most extravagant of evening Nobel wear. She introduced herself to the Entry Palace Guard and said, "I must speak with Queen Frella on an urgent family matter." Walking towards her gracefully and with attainment Cinderella smiled at her Stepmother. She expected her to plead for her salvation and speak for an exceeded period of time of the most utter and complete nonsense.

When Queen Frella approached the Duchess, she most superior in tone said, "Hello Stepmother." She curtsied proper in her elder presence. As she look up her Stepmother cunningly replied, "Hello... Cinderella."

— C.H.Darkling —

CHAPTER XV

"ROYAL ROOMMATES"

As she glare up at Stepmother with rage in her eyes; her silence was all the admission of guilt Stepmother needed. This time it *was* the wicked Stepmother who smiled with soft deceitful wiles.

"Let's retire to the Royal Courtyard shall we." Stepmother said most cordial. Cinderella nodded in agreement. She always worried of the day her and her Cinderboy got caught. However, she always had solace in knowing how easy she could rid herself of a servant. As they walked through the Palace to the leisure area of the courtyard, she kept her head down. For this was the least of her expectations for the day. She was wise enough to know her wicked stepmother's price for silence would be outrageous.

They sat down as if they were having a pleasant visit. Queen Frella immediately dismissed all Palace Guards that were near.

"Stepmother I love him! Time may be relentless along with status and rules...can't you see, only true love perseveres!" Cinderella pleaded. Stepmother just laughed for a good moment.

"True love? Oh, you stupid little girl! You will go through life wanting something you will never have." Stepmother replied merrily.

She immediately changed to a more pressing tone and said, "I have tried to accept you but... YOU DON'T LISTEN! Now see here, little girl, my daughters and I are residing in the Palace...today! And one of your more wise proclamations, as Queen, is to make your loving and intelligent Stepmother the new Royal Advisor. And I can promise you...you will NEVER be with William. On this matter tis nonnegotiable."

Cinderella knew she had no choice in that moment but to contain herself and agree, "Of course Stepmother." Cinderella dismissed herself quickly as knew she could not behead her Stepmother, with a large axe, as she so desired to right then. She silently walked away thinking to herself, "What was I thinking being a hostess to these intruders! That wicked old witch! She thinks she has me under her thumb. You might have succeeded in kicking me down Stepmother...but it won't last! For unlike *your* daughters...I'm just as wicked as you!" She was more than outraged and so desired her William to comfort her. But she knew she could not. And, viewing King Antonio as a "father figure", she somehow felt comfort in speaking with him.

His Majesty was enjoying himself in a game of Chess. Cinderella approached him with, "I love the game of Chess your Majesty! I am indeed most excellent in this...on and off the board." The King smiled and motioned his hand for her to sit and compete. "Of course you are your Highness; well then, by all means...proceed," he said. As she proceeded to make moves on the Chess board closer to beating King Antonio, she began to calm. She then spoke, "Your Royal Advisor's your Majesty. Are they still idiots at best?" King Antonio laughed and responded, "They are... I assume there is a reason for your asking my dear."

"Your Majesty you need trust and character surrounding you! NOT idiots. My stepmother is the wisest person I know. She is like my mother. I'm closer to her than her own daughters. She should indeed be Head Royal Advisor. She taught me how to play Chess my liege... and you're in check." Cinderella stated imperative. The King was shocked. Either no one before was wise enough to beat him...or brave.

"Very well your Highness," he replied.

"You won't regret this decision your Majesty! I'll have her and my two stepsisters sent here today!" Cinderella said as she pretended to be actually happy about this arrangement.

Stepmother was no fool. For evil knows evil. She knew her vicious stepdaughter would not let her stay in the lead for long. She thought it was time to stop shielding her own daughters and explain to them about "survival". She knew Ann would indeed need to partake in this seduction and scandal. For after the dethroned Queen Frella, it would be all the more easily to push Ann into Prince Alonso's arms. She then summoned for her two daughters.

As they enter the "Royal Advisors" quarters, Stepmother gave them no time to even breathe before attempting to convert her two daughters and bend them to her will. Fearing of what her evil stepdaughter's punishment may be; she panicked immediately and spoke, "Listen my darlings there's not much time. I have tried to protect you from the wickedness of your evil stepsister for some time now. Now that she's Queen, I can't do that. I know her surface seems sweet but she is evil in disguise. We must rid our family and this Kingdom of this horrid little girl. I promise to you...she is a monster." Ann was quick to inquire, "What can we do mother?"

Jezella starred in silence (for she had always seen through her mother more than Ann). Though naive in nature, she wondered why her mother was lying. "She has been more a sister to me than my own. Frella loves me for me and wishes for *me* to shine as I deserve… Unlike my mother." Jezella thought to herself.

Stepmother was all too happy to respond to Ann, "Dethrone this wicked Queen of course! I have shielded you from both the lies and darkness beneath this world around you. Now is the time for that to come to halt and for you two to learn of *survival*. For you are indeed future Royalty." Stepmother stated in all seriousness. "Now," she then changed to a more cavalier tone and said, "she is a lusty whore of a Queen. However, with her status and couth no one would believe that. I've been devising a plan, though, to frame her for poisoning the King."

Jezella and Ann both gasped in shock and fear. Jezella's heart almost fell out of her chest as she said, "Mother we cannot! We'd ALL be beheaded!"

"Calm yourself girls and silence your tongues! Now you listen to me." Their mother commanded them. "Frella's servants are loyal, beyond a doubt, to *her*. But Sir Fredrick's servants would be happy to see her burn I'm sure. We need a witness, not of our blood, to confirm our story."

The Duchess then took her daughter's close, looking at them directly in the eyes and said, "This family must stick together…do you understand?" Her daughters stood there in silence and fear. "If we stick together we can expose her and convince the Kingdom she tries to poison his Majesty to make her lover, Prince Alonso, king. It's a perfectly plausible plot acted out of lust for the crown." Stepmother said viciously.

"And Ann…as the Prince grieves over the loss of his sinister and greedy bride, I shall send you right into his arms. You will comfort him and show him your kindness and grace. However, you must also...inform him he married the WRONG sister!" She told her daughter (with a little *too* much joy, as if she'd gone mad). "We shall convene in the morning. We need not raise suspicion," she said.

Ann too kind and innocent in nature knew not what to do or say. She nodded in agreement completely and utterly shocked beyond believe at her mother. Jezella just put her head down and dismissed herself.

— *100* —

— *C.H.Darkling* —

CHAPTER XVI

"CHECK MATE"

Jezella knew no what to do or say she thought to herself, "I cannot betray the King and risk my life but how could I betray the mother who raised me?" She then thought to herself, "Perhaps if I *do* tell my stepsister, she will have mercy on mother and no one else need to know. Queen Frella is and above all others and loves me and will have mercy. I must tell her to save this family!" She knew her sister Ann would be too frightened to go against her mother. Jezella was of course frightened as well; her and her sister could *both* clearly see (for once) their mother's sickness of the mind. Jezella finally came to the conclusion, her mother had gone mad and that she must tell her stepsister!

She knew not what to say as she walked closer to the Queen's quarters. She tried to think of how to break it to her gently that her own mother was wickedly plotting against Frella. So being the little halfwit she was, as Cinderella called her to enter she immediately started yelling.

"Oh sister she has gone mad! My mother has finally gone completely mad! I always knew my mother was no Saint...but she has become wicked. I'm so sorry sister. Something has come over her and she plans to dethrone you!" Cinderella could see that her minion had valuable information and was hysterical.

"Calm down my sister, it's alright. You know I love Stepmother...exactly what happened?" Cinderella tried to soothe her and find out Stepmother's exact plans so she could seize them. Jezella started to cry and said, "Have mercy on her Frella for her mind is obviously not right."

"Of course sister. You can trust me. Just tell me please." Cinderella said gently.

"She has it in her trusted head that you are evil. I don't know why. Perhaps she is jealous that you are Queen and not Ann. But, she is planning to kill his Majesty! And...blaming you for it! We will all be beheaded! Frella you must not tell anyone please! What do we do?" Jezella said frightfully.

Cinderella was shocked. Her stepmother's wickedness ran deeper than she expected. She automatically knew she must "eliminate ALL threats". She also knew that, in that moment, she must calm her stupid stepsister. For her "Royal Plans" to eliminate Stepmother were so bad, she couldn't even begin to think of her vengeance. "Blinded by the ways of her mother, I must distract her from interfering with my plans," Cinderella thought to herself. She then looked at Jezella, most sincere and said, "You are my only family left little sister. I love you most dear and shall reward you for your loyalty! You are saving this Kingdom. I shall see you marry well to the most gorgeous, lusty Prince I can find. And don't worry about Mother. I will handle this situation delicately and with caution!"

As Cinderella screamed to the top of her lungs, she thought of all the sinister ways to brutally murder Stepmother...and enjoy it. "You wicked witch!" Cinderella shout. She then thought to herself, "If I am to be punished Stepmother for my treacheries...than you shall be punished too!" Her first thought was too behead the evil, with a LARGE axe! She also fantasized (and with joy) about slitting Stepmother's throat and appreciating the blood run down her neck. "It's time the world be rid of you Stepmother!" She thought aloud (as she wished more than anything she could burn the witch). She cared no more of suspicion at this moment as she *needed* to see William. She immediately had Drake escort her straight to her Cinderboy's and Royal Taylor's Quarter's.

Cinderella could contain her emotions not as she ran into her William's arms and burst into tears (something she did not do often).

"She knows my love! She knows! We must kill her! We are doomed!" Cinderella cried to him.

"Whom?!" William inquired eagerly.

"Stepmother!" Cinderella shrieked. William's eyes widened with shock. "She somehow found out about us! She has forced her way into the Palace and intended on dethroning me! She must die! There's no time to spare! William we must kill her!" Cinderella proclaimed.

Her Cinderboy held her. He kissed her forehead, so gentle, so soft as he rubbed her hair back and attempted to comfort his love.

"Frella, your clouded by your hate for her! You act hasty when you get angry this way my love. You are Queen now. You cannot act as you are mad! You must think before you make your next move on the Chessboard...like you taught me." William said soothingly.

"Your absolutely right my darling!" Cinderella replied as she finally began to calm. "William, regardless of how we plan these affairs, she must die... Soon! She is a threat that must be eliminated once and for all! Before she eliminates *us* my love!" Cinderella spoke intently.

"Frella you cannot," William shook his head and spoke. "They are your family. You cannot *KILL* your stepmother! There must be another way. You are the Queen at punishing people my love!" He yelled at her. She was most certainly in not point and time in the mood to hear her lover's (over-excessive) virtues. She was, in that moment, truly disgusted with his moral pro quo. The only word that actually triggered something in her wicked mind was "family".

She then put her hand over her Cinderboy's mouth to silence him. She then spoke aloud, "Family! Yes! They are my family. And by dismantling that, I shall cut off her wicked black wings!" William with most curiosity spoke, "My love you're speaking in circles once more." Cinderella then replied, "Her disappearance can easily be explained by her 'leaving to secure allies'. After all... isn't that what the Royal Advisor should be concerned of?" William spout, "Royal Advisor?!" with most curiosity.

Again Cinderella covered her lover's mouth to silence him. "William keep pace please, this is no game!" she snarled. "If I marry off *both* 'my sisters', we can secure allies! Not to mention, I will be depriving Stepmother's fire of its coal." Cinderella said imperative. "I will then enjoy stabbing my attacker as we leave word she journeyed to Norway to formalize a Peace Treaty. It's Brilliant! We will be unstoppable if we succeed my darling!" Cinderella said serenely.

Her gorgeous and sexy true love then began to kiss her. He gently moved his soft hands down from fondling her hair to her breasts. Cinderella was seduced (as usual) by William's gentle touch. As her loins began to burn for him, she needed him to "put her fire out". She kissed him back lustfully. He began to bite her neck, knowing it put her in a hypnotic state of eroticism. She then pushed his body back to definitely straddle him (for she had en-joyed being the "more dominate one" with her Prince). William then took off his shirt as he rubbed his hands up her Royal dress eager to put his cock in her.

She scurried to rip off her undergarments as she rammed his cock inside her. She needed his touch. She rocked her hips rapidly back and forth. She more rapidly rode his cock up and down as her moister spilled all over it. She kissed him with passion riding him harder and faster until her eyes rolled back. She moaned sensuous as she was about to finish. William then whispered in her ear, "Promise me you will not brutally murder her my love." Cinderella then bit his neck and pulled his body close. She scratched down his body as she "promised".

If William had been looking in her eyes at that mo-ment...he would have seen the evil in them. He would have seen the true sin her grin...for it was an enormous lie. Cinderella passionately kissed William as he spilled his seed in her. However, she quickly dismissed her-self for she had much "Royal Plans" to attend to (and was more than displeased her lover would not be part of them). But as I said, she was a determined girl. She knew she could always rely on her loyal servant Drake.

As he escorted his Queen to her Royal Quarters she whispered intently to him, "You will enter my cham-bers as everyone sleeps. We have most dangerous liai-sons to attend to. Have your brother stand guard as we have much to discuss." Cinderella wasted no time going straight to her writing desk as she enter her quarters and began writing Stepmother's "Goodbye Letter".

Your Majesty,

I am most happy to hear of my two darling daughters marrying into prestigious Royal Families and binding allies to this Kingdom. I am writing you this letter to prove myself worthy of my place as your Head Royal Advisor. For as your reading this message, I am traveling North to acquire a legal Peace Treaty with King Albert. I apologize for my hasty decision. However, when I return from my crusade...we will be a Kingdom united by all!

Sincerely,
The Duchess of Frey
Your Royal Advisor

CHAPTER XVII

"THE BITTER END"

As Cinderella arose the next morning and enjoyed her Royal Steam Bath she knew she must send her loving Prince Alonso on a wild goose chase today; and keep him as far away from her murderous agenda as possible. For she could have NO distractions and NO mistakes if she were to succeed.

You see, late last night while the moon was high, our Dark Cinderella had already discussed with her beloved Stable Boys the details of Stepmother's demise. She had already discussed with the younger brother Alejandro, his part in readying the Royal carriage to dispose of the body and hightailing to the river. They had, of course, discussed if he were questioned that he was delivering a Peace Offering to Norway in the name of Queen Frella. And it's no surprise, her Royal Bodyguard and Stable Boy #1, Drake, would indeed stand guard outside Stepmother's quarters. He would indeed be ready to roll her corpse into a fine rug, wrapped in fine silk garments, disguised as "fine gifts" for King Albert of Norway.

She had already sent word (through her dress maid) for Jezella to meet her at high noon. She knew her minion would help her do anything to save the King and her mother from self-destruction. She could be counted upon, surely, to intervene with the King's poisoning attempt. Yes, as she tried to clear her anxieties Cinderella had already had much discussions. She had already requested a glass of wine...and she had already sharpened her blade. (It was a beautiful dagger her father's oldest friend, Sir Alexander Smith, had given her after an expedition.)

As she approached her Prince's quarters, she knew to send him on a few days journey to quire goods from neighboring Kingdoms and keep him out of her way. Prince Alonso would, of course, not deny his new bride's request to "gain Royal favor" among surrounding Kingdoms. However, dismissing her dark and sexy husband was the least of Cinderella's worries today.

She knew not of details when it came to Royal Suiters to marry her stepsister's to. She knew her throne would be secure, once she showed King Antonio her "Knowledge of Chess" by securing allies. Cinderella began to think to herself, "His Majesty will be pleased with the 'aspiration of success' this new family has... But how can I convince him to stay silenced of such a grand union until *I* announce to Stepmother her defeat? How can I halt such an announcement?" Cinderella was at a standstill.

She was in much turbulence as the wheels in her wicked little head kept turning. She then uttered, "I need a very 'large' distraction for the ENTIRE Palace whilst I vanquish Stepmother!" Then it came to her... "Every loves a party! If the new Queen were to order a Royal Banquet, the Royal Servants would be in a complete frenzy preparing! The Royal Court (as well as King Antonio) would be distracted, much concerned with 'fashions and appearances' for the event! I can silence King Antonio easily by suggesting a 'Royal Banquet' to celebrate our Kingdom's expansions. He would not question that *I* (as Queen) would like to make the announcement to *my* stepsisters. It's perfect! I shall leave no noose untied while I conspire to hang my enemies." Cinderella thought to herself.

Cinderella explained to Jezella "that all would be forgiven" and remain "in the family" as long as she pretended to partake in her mother's plan and ensure the poison be disposed of, long before reaching the King. She then scurried to approach his Majesty with her "Royal Plans".

As Cinderella's Royal Guards announced "The Queen's" presence to King Antonio in the Royal Headquarters, she ordered ALL the servants dismissal as well. This made King Antonio well aware he and his new daughter-in-law had much to discuss. She waltz towards him most superior and said, "King Antonio, I am here as your Queen to announce your new Royal Advisor's first proclamation to surround our entire Kingdom with protection, wealth and loyalty your Majesty."

"That sounds like every King's dream, dear. And I am not surprised any plot out of *your* mouth." King Antonio giggled at her always charmed by her honesty and boldness. He changed to a more sarcastic tone, thinking the girl was dreaming and said, "Frella, how do you plan to accomplish this?"

"That is simple your Majesty, for my stepmother has taught me to play Chess *very* well as you remember. You see, before my marriage to your son... Spain only had gold and trades to bargain with. But now you haven't just acquired one new daughter...you've acquired three! And they are both stunning beauties I might add. Stepmother says you must *bind* your enemies to you to secure allies. So tell me your Majesty, whom is an available suiter to the East and West to marry my darling sisters to?" Cinderella stated most narcissistic.

She grinned most domineering and devious to King Antonio. She enjoyed spending time with a new "father figure" she had much in common with. Unlike her real father, King Antonio was impressed with her strategies (not appalled by manipulation). He overjoyed smiled back at the new Queen as the two consulted and connived together.

"The only available unity to the West is King Marcelo of Brazil. King Marcelo is a widower, however, unattractive and undesirable as they come. He is more than twice your stepsister's age. Frella, are you certain this can be successful?" King Antonio inquired.

"My eldest and most beautiful sister Ann is as kind and wise as her mother. She would be more understanding this marriage is essential to this Kingdom for she is most humble. And I'm sure a lonely old king would no doubtibly be susceptible to Ann's beauty. But your Majesty... Is it at all possible at least one of my sisters could possibly find love, like I did with your son?" Cinderella replied.

"Oh your Highness...you do have a heavy heart made out of gold. My dear Isabella would have loved you!" stated King Antonio. His Majesty stewed, however. Cinderella refused quite a few of the Eastern Suiters until Prince Riccolo of Aragon was mentioned. For starters, his reputation of being charming and handsome got her attention. She didn't like breaking promises to Loyal Servants and Jezella was one of them. Cinderella was woman of her word when it came to holding up her end of a deal. She knew he'd be the perfect reward for Jezella.

However, what Cinderella was most aware of was; the younger the man...the easier to educate. Cinderella was slightly uncertain when King Antonio mentioned his well-known promiscuities. But then she realized, he would ignorant never-the-less. After all, the younger the bull...the easier to tame!

"He sounds perfect for Jezella your Majesty!" Cinderella interrupted. "For we now have an age old tested weapon." She patiently waited for King Antonio to inquire, "What?" Cinderella changed to a cold and severe tone (like a true leader) and replied, "For it will be easy for this new Royal Family to succeed in this endeavor."

"Your Grace... May I suggest a Royal Banquet for dinner this evening to make the announcement to my sisters? Let's waste no time informing our Royal Court and Advisors of this Kingdom's future success and security!" Cinderella requested charmingly. She knew she had King Antonio wrapped around her fingers as she did her father as he was obviously proud of her.

"Lovely idea your Highness. You can properly inform your stepsisters then." King Antonio replied. He then proceeded to ask her, "Has my son been informed of the future of this Kingdom Frella?" Cinderella knew Prince Alonso could not be present for the banquet and get in her way today.

"I'll tell my husband now your Grace." Cinderella replied and quickly dismissed herself. She knew she must hurry and send him off before the King had a chance to see him. She then hurried to rid herself of Prince Alonso having her final discussion of the day.

She then said to herself, "See you at the bitter end Stepmother" as she had completed all preparations for the final battle of this war. She had ALL the Royal Servants in a state of frenzy as she scurried to her quarters to dress properly for a "proper conversation" with her stepmother before dinner. And she had, of course, sent her servant Drake to stand guard and patrol the area around her stepmother's quarters. As Cinderella drew nigh to them she had nothing on her mind but her enemy's blood. She was more than ready to have an "honest conversation with Stepmother...for once. (Pleased at the thought of her being buried with it.)

Cinderella began to slow her pace as she approached the last hallway to Stepmother's quarters. And she could not help but to think, "How could the love and light of my life be the person I'm hiding my most grave intentions to?" She then thought to herself, "She threatens ALL. How could he *ever* be against me ending her?! That imbecile! Sometimes I wonder why we love each other so. For William is indeed my greatest weakness!" As she get closer and closer to Stepmother's door, preparing herself for a gruesome and vicious kill, she came to a realization, "How could I have been so senseless as to not see it before! How could I not comprehend...that *My Cinderboy* is indeed my ultimate competitor in this Game of Chess!"

Cinderella felt enlightened as she entered her Stepmother's room. She felt guiltless and free to show her true colors as she announce her enemy's defeat.

"Hello Stepmother." She said so sweet it was sickening. Stepmother most malicious replied, "Hello... Cinderella".

"It's Queen Frella!" Cinderella snapped. She then walked closer to her stepmother and sarcastically, spitefully snarled, "You know I've prayed to God I can think of a kind thing to say Stepmother, but I cannot." Stepmother smiled and silently shrugged.

Cinderella then delighted to "cut her stepmother's wicked wings off" and announce Sweet Ann's engagement to the elderly and ugly King of Brazil. Stepmother was, of course, outraged at the idea and was quick to scold Cinderella.

"You are nothing but a spoiled and spiteful little girl! You always have been…and underneath your crown, a cinderboy's whore!" Stepmother proclaimed. Cinderella shrieked back at her, practically growling, and said, "You Bitch! I wish I could show the world your wickedness!" Stepmother immediately giggled and replied, "Then they'd see your wickedness as well, little girl. For your soul is blacker than mine could ever be."

Cinderella then tore up as she drew closer and closer to Stepmother. She actually shed sincere tears (for once) for she knew Stepmother spoke the truth.

She began to whisper to her stepmother, "On the Devil's list in hell is your name Stepmother." As she had discreetly been reaching for the dagger the whole time, (within the blink of an eye) she swiftly stabbed the dagger upward into Stepmother's ribs with ALL her might. As Stepmother's eyes became bloodshot and bulged out of her head, Cinderella covered her mouth and twisted the blade. She then quickly pulled the dagger out as Stepmother fell to the floor. Her wound was pouring blood as Cinderella put her heel right on her Stepmother's throat to speed up the assassination. As she enjoyed watching the witch suffocate, she enjoyed watching the blood of her conquered enemy dripping off her dagger more!

As she watched it drip she had a feeling of accomplishment and true serenity. She enjoyed the moment and removed her heel from Stepmother's throat. Cinderella then casually wiped off her weapon and said, "You know the good thing about cinders Stepmother? Hmmm? They can easily be washed off!" She then looked down at the blood surging out of the gruesome puncture in Stepmother's body so that it made a puddle.

As she much enjoyed watching Stepmother take her

dying breathes she looked desperate to have last words with her. Cinderella couldn't help but to curiously kneel down...

As the Duchess was gasping her last breathes she said, "I would have loved you dear Frella. You *are* like me and I wanted to accept you as my own. I'm so sorry." Her voice crackled as she cried and gasped deeper. She then took Cinderella's hand upon her last breath and said, "But I was only wicked...after you."

INDEX

PREFACE	5
INTRODUCTION TO CHARACTERS	7
CHAPTER I "INTRODUCTIONS"	17
CHAPTER II "THE PARTY"	23
CHAPTER III "LEGALITIES AND FUN"	29
CHAPTER IV "THE DEATH"	35
CHAPTER V "THE HOSTILE TAKEOVER"	39
CHAPTER VI "THE PRINCE"	47
CHAPTER VII "THE CINDERBOY"	55
CHAPTER VIII "ANN'S PURE HEART"	61
CHAPTER IX "ROYAL SEDUCTION"	65
CHAPTER X "ROYAL INTRODUCTIONS"	71
CHAPTER XI "THE ROYAL WEDDING PART 1"	75
CHAPTER XII "THE ROYAL WEDDING PART 2"	79
CHAPTER XIII "A WICKED REIGN"	85
CHAPTER XIV "BATTLE ROYAL"	91
CHAPTER XV "ROYAL ROOMMATES"	95
CHAPTER XVI "CHECK MATE"	101
CHAPTER XVII "THE BITTER END"	107
INDEX	115